Marlow:
LOST
GIRL

A Key West Mystery

MARLOW
LOST GIRL
BILL CRAIG

A Key West Mystery

BILL CRAIG

ABSOLUTELY AMAZING eBOOKS

ABSOLUTELY AMAZING eBOOKS

*To all of those who lost lives
and property to Hurricane Irma
when she hit Florida.*

*Also, for Meghan who
graciously allowed her face
to decorate this cover!*

Marlow: LOST GIRL

A Key West Mystery

Chapter One

Quinn Kerns struggled with the ropes binding her wrists to the arms of the chair. Her wrists were bleeding from where the rough strands had bitten into her tender skin. She wanted to scream, but the duct tape over her mouth took that ability away from her, too!

Tears flowed from her eyes and ran down her cheeks. All she had wanted was to get away from her father. Especially, since he had started molesting her. Key West had sounded fun and exotic, like a good place to turn into somebody else.

Nobody had warned her about how crazy things were. Or that a category five hurricane would hit the island not long after she got there. Nobody had warned her that evil lurked in the shadows of paradise, like that mythical serpent hiding in the Garden of Eden. Quinn shook her head and tried to breath more than a snuffle since her nose was getting clogged up from crying. Somebody would find her eventually, but it was up to her to make she that she stayed alive long enough for that to happen!

Quinn shivered as a chill raced down her spine. She had to try and get free. One way or another. There was no way that she would let this fucking nutcase kill her. She kept working her hands against the ropes. Maybe, if she bled enough, she would be able to slip through the ropes.

~ ~ ~

Like many others, one week after the devastating storm, Rick Marlow had been conscripted to help haul away debris left over from Hurricane Irma. Tina was busy working in 'Pepe's'. The heat and humidity was getting to him, but that was really nothing new. The island community had been hard hit by Irma.

Marlow was lending a hand, trying to help everyone that had been impacted by the hurricane. So, as he was helping cut up a falling tree, he was surprised to feel his cell phone vibrating in his pocket. He pulled it out and answered it. "Marlow."

"Ricky, I need you to come back to the office right away," Walter Loomis told him.

"Okay, Walter, I'm on my way," Marlow told his boss. He looked over at Jack Marsh. "Jack, I'm sorry, but the boss wants me. I hate to leave you in the lurch."

"Go, Rick. We'll manage," Marsh told him.

"I figured," Marlow said with a wave. He wondered what was so important for Walter to call him away. As he as headed to Walter's house, he saw Finn Pilar and his three-legged dog, Crutch, on a street corner. Marlow grinned. Crutch was rapidly becoming a favorite around town with his antics.

~ ~ ~

Marlow parked his bicycle in the rack and locked it in place before he entered through his outside office door. He grabbed a bottle of ice water from his mini fridge and then headed down the hall to the conference room that Walter worked out of.

A woman in her forties sat at the table with Walter.

Marlow walked in and took a seat, twisting the cap off his bottle of water. He took a long pull at it while waiting for Walter to acknowledge him.

"Ah, Ricky, so good of you to join us," Walter smiled.

"Well, I've been kind of busy helping out around town with the clean up after Irma."

"And your help is greatly appreciated. Irma was a fierce storm to say the least. However, Mrs. Kerns has need of your regular services," Walter explained.

"A case?" Marlow leaned forward.

"My daughter ran away. She was coming here to get away from my soon to be ex-husband. She thought she could make a fresh start, away from us. I haven't heard from her since," Marla Kerns explained.

"Do you have a recent picture?" Marlow asked. He knew that he would need it to show around to see if anybody had seen her.

"Yes," Mrs. Kerns said as she dug into her purse. She pulled one out and handed it to him. The daughter was fifteen years old but looked older. Her expression in the picture looked haunted. Marlow wondered about that. He tucked the picture into his shirt pocket.

"So, tell me more about Quinn," Marlow told her.

"Quinn used to be a happy girl. Full of life and laughter. Then, about six months ago, all that changed. She was quiet, secretive, her grades started to fall at school," Marla explained.

"Did you suspect that she was being molested?" Marlow asked.

"I wondered, but I couldn't get her to talk to me. After she disappeared, I found her diary and I kicked my husband out of the house. Quinn is my everything."

"So, then she left, and you weren't sure where she had gone?

"No, not at first. But finally, one of her friends told me that she had talked about coming down here and starting over."

"Do you know if she had any friends down here? Or any family members?"

"None that I am aware of, Mr. Marlow," Marla replied with a sigh.

"Finding a juvenile on the streets of Key West won't be easy, Mrs. Kerns. But I will do my best. I'm sure Walter has already gone over my retainer and had you sign a contract?

"He has, and he has the check I wrote."

"As soon as the check clears the bank I'll start looking for Quinn," Marlow said.

"That's a better response than I have got from the police, both back home and here," Marla sighed.

~ ~ ~

After Marla Kerns had left, Marlow returned to the conference room and took his regular seat across from Walter. Since his heart attack, Lola his secretary had made it a point to make sure the old man was eating better and exercising on a regular basis. Now Walter was down thirty pounds and had a renewed vigor about him. "Why were you so quick to accept this case?" Marlow asked him curiously.

"Things have been slow since Irma hit. Plus, I am very worried about this girl," Walter replied.

"You think she might have been on the island when Irma hit," Marlow said, it wasn't a question.

"I think so," Walter admitted, running his hands

through his snow-white hair, pushing it back from his face.

"If she was, she might not have made it. This puts things in new light. I'll start looking right away," Marlow told his boss, standing and taking the picture. He would scan it and print off copies in his own office at the end of the hall.

"Thank you, Ricky," Walter said as Marlow headed into the hall. When he reached his office, Marlow booted up his computer first thing. He also turned on his printer-scanner. Opening his browser, Marlow typed in the name Quinn Kerns and hit enter. He would do more specific database searches later, but since she was young and probably active on social media, he wanted to check social media sites first.

In seconds, he came up with hits on Facebook, Instagram, Snapchat, and Twitter. He began clicking on each link. It took him nearly an hour to work through each page on each site. She has made her last posts the day Irma had hit before the cell towers went down.

Marlow leaned back in his chair, contemplating the computer screen. Her mother had been right about the molestation. Quinn had posted about it to some of her friends. Why hadn't the cops in Marathon looked into it? That was a question for another day. Right now, he was more interested in finding the girl. One of her last posts said that she had found a job. She had also mentioned renting a small apartment in a rooming house, but she didn't say which one.

Marlow picked up the telephone and dialed Thom Hark at the Key West Citizen newspaper. "Thom Hark speaking."

"Thom, are you free for lunch at the 'Chart Room Bar'?" Marlow asked, naming the restaurant where he had first met the intrepid reporter.

"On who's dime?" Hark asked.

"I'm buying."

"Of course, I'm free, Rick. When would you like to meet?"

"About half an hour from now?" Marlow asked.

"I'll see you there," Thom replied and hung up. Marlow shook his head. He made copies of Quinn Kearns picture and printed them out. Later, he would use one of the programs to make fliers with her picture and put them up around town.

Like Walter, Marlow was now very worried about what had happened to Quinn Kerns. Bad things had a way of happening to young girls, especially in South Florida. A lot of it had to do with the transient population, but some of it was because there were just bad people out there who wouldn't think twice about taking advantage of someone young and vulnerable. Marlow took a copy of the picture of Quinn and headed out the door.

He unlocked his bicycle from the rack and peddled to the 'Chart Room Bar'. He locked his bike up there and went inside, finding a table. Thom Hark joined him moments later. "Ricky my friend, what can I do for you," Thom asked tilting back a bottle of Budweiser.

"I'm looking for a teenage girl, a runaway that got here shortly before Irma hit. She's disappeared," Marlow explained. Thom's face was suddenly serious. His own sister had died at the hands of a serial killer back in England.

"Tell me more," Thom said, all traces of geniality vanished. He could smell a story in the making.

"Her name is Quinn Kerns and she ran away from home.

Apparently, after her father began molesting her. She arrived shortly before Irma hit, but hasn't been seen or heard from since. Her last social media postings came the day Irma hit," Marlow explained.

"Do you have a picture? This is something that I could run in the newspaper," Thom said.

"I was hoping you would say that," Marlow pulled a copy of her picture out of one of the cargo pockets of his shorts and slid it across the table. Thom picked it up and looked at it.

"She does look familiar, but I can't say where I might have seen her. However, I will get this out in the paper and will keep an eye out for her."

"I appreciate it, Thom." Marlow looked up as the waitress arrived to take their order. They both ordered hotdogs and Marlow ordered a Margarita to accompany his.

"Starting early, aren't you?" Thom asked.

"It's been one of those days. Besides, Tina is up north visiting her mother for a week. I get to be decadent this week," Marlow grinned.

"What is your next stop on this case, Rick?" Thom asked.

"I've made up fliers and I plan on putting them up all over town. If Quinn was here, someone has to have seen her. They might even be able to tell me the last place that they saw her. At this point, anything helps," Marlow shrugged.

"I'm sure that it does," Thom agreed. He agreed to write up the story and to let Marlow look it over before printing it. Marlow paid the check after they ate and the two men parted ways. Marlow made his way back to the office. After locking his bike up, he went back on line and started searching special databases for people in his line of work.

~ ~ ~

Lost Girl

He had made sure to clean up after himself before returning to work. He had to be very careful so that nobody would find out what he had done. Oscar had told him that was the best way to do things. Oscar was his boss, so he listened to him.

Oscar was a lot smarter than he was. He always had been. That was why he always did what Oscar told him to do. Oscar took care of him. He always had. He loved Oscar, because Oscar was his big brother and Oscar had promised that he would always take care of him!

~ ~ ~

Walter and Lola had retired upstairs to Walter's private apartment by the time that Marlow had returned to his office. He was inclined to let the two of them have their privacy. Their secret romance was one of the worst kept secrets on the rock. Especially to Marlow who knew both of them on an almost intimate fashion.

Marlow took the fliers that he had printed out and headed out, this time taking his car, a 2003 Ford Escape. He headed for home first. Once there, he would feed his cat and then eat. After that, he would start hanging the fliers all around town. Finding Quinn Kearns was now his number one priority!

~ ~ ~

It was night by the time that he hit Duval Street. Despite the remains of Irma, the place was packed with tourists. Marlow posted fliers all over town. He wanted to find this girl. He wanted to find her badly.

Chapter Two

Duval Street was business as usual once the sun went down. People came to what was known as the End of the Road to get away from it all. That was a given. So, Marlow was there, waiting for somebody to make a move.

He had been up and down the street, posting fliers on utility poles and in each of the bars. Sooner or later, he was sure that he would get a hit. Key West was a small island. Somebody would have seen the girl. It was just a matter of time before he found out who.

Kids flocked to Key West looking to party and have fun. Some stayed, some didn't. Some disappeared without a trace, even when a hurricane hadn't blown through a few weeks before. "Hey, Marlow, where have you been?" Steve Lorca asked, appearing out of the crowds that were moving up and down Duval. Marlow had met Lorca while helping with clean up around the island.

Lorca was ex-Navy and had decided to stay on the rock after he had gotten out. He spent most of his time working on boats in the Bight. But after Irma, everybody on the island pitched in to help everyone else. It was just that kind of community.

"Hey, Steve, have you seen this girl?" Marlow asked, handing him one of the flyers. Lorca looked down and studied the picture of the young girl's picture. He shook his head no.

"I can't say that I have, Rick. She has a face that I am pretty sure I'd remember," Lorca told him.

"I appreciate you taking a look. Can you keep an eye out for her while you're helping with the clean up?"

"I can do that, pal. Make sure you relax some, okay? All work and no play, know what I mean?"

"Yes, I do. Good seeing you," Marlow told him, heading on down Duval towards the alley that led to the 'Smokin' Tuna Saloon'. He's stopped in at the 'Red Garter Bar', too, but he didn't hold much hope of finding anything useful there. Strippers were notoriously closed-mouthed about talking to anybody with a badge. Even P.I.'s.

But Charlie would let him post one of the flyers there. It wasn't much, but it was something. Still, he had an itch in the center of his back. Somebody was watching him. But why? Did it have to do with Quinn Kearns and the flyers that he was putting up?

Marlow slowed down, using the reflective qualities of the glass in the many shops and bars along the street to check his back trail as best as he could. Whoever was following him was good. Really good. Marlow turned the corner by the 'Red Garter'. Maybe he could pick them out if they followed him all the way to the Tuna.

A live band that Marlow didn't recognize was playing on the outside stage. Marlow headed for the outside bar that bordered another alley and ordered a Bud. "Is Charlie around?" he asked the bartender. This was a new girl.

"Inside," she replied taking his money for the beer before he left the counter and headed for the indoor bar.

Charlie was near the door when Marlow entered. So much the better.

"Charlie, how have you been?" Marlow asked the owner, Charlie Bauer.

"Good, Rick. You?" Bauer asked.

"I survived Irma. So, I guess pretty good."

"I'm gonna have that put on a tee shirt," Charlie laughed.

"I bet you'll sell a bunch. You ever see this girl? She's around sixteen or so," Marlow asked.

"I don't know her, but that doesn't mean she hasn't been here," Charlie shrugged.

"I get that. Will you put it up, so the employees can see it? I'm willing to pay for information," Marlow told him.

"She a runaway?"

"Yeah, she is. She came here before Irma. I'm trying to find out if she survived."

"I get that," Charlie nodded. "The storm was a bad one. Did you take this to the cops?" Charlie asked.

"Not yet, but I plan to," Marlow told him.

"Do it sooner than later than later, Rick. A girl like her, some guys would pick her up and sell her without thinking twice."

"I know that, Charlie. That is exactly what I am trying to prevent," Marlow told him.

"I hope you can, Rick. I'll have everybody take a look at the flyers and hang them on the doors and beside the bars. Good Luck." Marlow handed him a few of the flyers and headed back towards Duval.

The sky was cloudy when he got back to Duval Street and it was starting to get dark. Thunder rumbled overhead.

Great, just what the island needed, another storm. Marlow headed for Mallory Square, though he had a feeling that it would be emptying out pretty fast as he watched lightning spear across the sky. If worse came to worse, he could stop by Tina's apartment and spend the night there. She had given him a key a long time ago.

The first fat drops of rain started to fall as he made his way past the stages that line the side of 'Maison De Pepe's' in Old Town Key West. Mallory Square had started emptying of the few hardy souls that had come out after staying through Irma. Marlow could understand the need. The majority of Conch's residents had hunkered down and rode it out, and they had a little cabin fever and knew that their friends and neighbors needed help with the cleanup. He was trotting along the sidewalk towards Tina's apartment building when something hit the back of his head, putting his lights out.

~ ~ ~

Quinn opened her eyes. She must have passed out. She could hear another storm outside. Thunder so loud that it shook the house around her. Her wrists hurt where she had torn them open against the rope that bound her to the wooden chair. How could she have been so stupid? When the cute guy offered to let her ride out the storm at his place, she should have been cautious and asked if anyone else was going there. But she hadn't. She had just gone with him because he had seemed so nice. And look where that had gotten her. Quinn shook her head, fighting back more tears.

She had tried to get away when he grabbed her once they were inside the house, but he was bigger and stronger. It hurt when he raped her, even worse than the first time her father had done it. He beat her when she fought him. He had won that fight as well, punching her until she was unconscious. She had awakened tied to the chair with no clothes on.

This guy was a sick bastard. It made her wonder if he had done this before to other naïve and unsuspecting young girls. Probably not the riding out the hurricane bit, but some other lure to get them inside his place. She shivered at the thought, wondering what other horrors awaited her!

~ ~ ~

He snuck through the house not making any noise. The storm frightened him. It wasn't as bad as the big one that had blown through. Oscar had told him not to worry, that the house was built to withstand the great big storms like the last one. But the thunder was so loud that it scared him.

Oscar had told him not to go into the room where she was. But she was pretty, and he liked her. He had enjoyed being with her after Oscar had got done. She didn't even know about him. He licked his lips, wondering if maybe he could have her before Oscar got home. He licked his lips again. Then he heard the front door open and headed back towards it. Oscar would be mad if he found out that he had tried to look at the girl again.

He didn't want to make Oscar mad. Oscar hit him when he was mad. It hurt when Oscar beat him. He didn't like that. No, that was not fun at all. It was better if he just did what Oscar told him to do.

~ ~ ~

It was still raining when Marlow opened his eyes. His face hurt, and his head hurt. He managed to push himself up into a sitting position before the world started spinning even more. It was dark on this side of the building. Nobody was at the glass bottom boat tours. The boat was still gone. He had no idea where it had been taken to ride out Irma. Marlow leaned back against the brick wall of the apartment building. He checked his hip. His revolver was still there. That was something at least. It wasn't until he had climbed up the wall that he realized that the remaining flyers were gone. He looked around. They were nowhere to be seen.

Why had his attacker taken them? It was a puzzle. Apparently, he had frightened somebody by posting the flyers. Was it because they had Quinn Kerns? Or because they had killed her? He frowned as the rain continued to soak him to the skin. There were to goddam many questions and no answers. At least, not yet.

Still, he had shaken somebody up. The question was who? He figured that the answer would wait until morning as he stumbled along to the front of the building and made his way to Tina's apartment. Marlow let himself in and stripped off his wet clothes. He turned the shower on, letting the spray heat up, and then he climbed in and let it warm him up.

Afterwards he toweled himself dry and pulled on a pair of athletic shorts that he kept there. Wearing them, he made his way to the kitchen. He didn't bother with beer tonight. Instead he grabbed the fifth of vodka and poured himself half a glass. He added some cranberry-pineapple juice to it. He walked to the living room, put some Art Pepper on the audio player. He took a sip as he leaned back into the couch and closed his eyes.

The music flowed over him as he thought about the day's events. He was sure that Quinn Kearns was still alive.

At least at the moment. The question was, could he find her before she wasn't? Marlow took another sip. It tasted too damn good to sip. He drank it down, then went to the kitchen and made himself another.

He thought about calling the cops, but the chief was still dealing with fallout from everything that had gone on during the hunt for the lost Hemingway manuscript[1]. Marlow shook his head. Chief Jamie Gutierrez was slowly surely getting back in the good graces of the city council and Marlow didn't want to do anything to mess that up. Midnight Blues was still open, but Marlow didn't know for how long. It had been a hard thing for Jamie when Elise had given him an ultimatum about being a cop. They had broken each other's hearts.

It had been a sad thing for him to watch. Sad for Tina, too. He missed her right now. But she had gone to visit her family and to testify against Kurt Dawes' brother for impersonating and allowing his twin to come to come to Florida to stalk and try to kill Tina[2]. He missed her terribly, but he was also concerned about her safety. The Chicago Police Department hadn't done such a good job of protecting her from Kurt Dawes. So, he didn't trust them to do a great job this time either.

Though Jack Riley had put some calls back to his old department to make sure that Tina would have round the clock protection while she was there. It would have to do. With luck, Tina would be home by early next week and they could start making plans for Christmas. Marlow smiled at

---

[1] Papa's Legacy
[2] Something Wicked

the thought as he added more vodka to his glass. His head was still tender from where he had been hit, but he was pretty sure that he didn't have a concussion. A slow warmth was spreading through his body as the alcohol worked its way into his system. He turned on the television and flipped through the channels, finally settling on a station that was showing the old black and white version of 'Casablanca'. It was one of his favorite movies. And while he appreciated the colorized version, the original black and white was the best. He finished the vodka and was soon snoring on the couch.

He hadn't counted on anybody to come looking for the girl. That hadn't been part of the plan at all. Runaways came to 'the rock' all the time. Some hung around, some disappeared. Quinn acted like that there would be nobody that would care if she were missing. He had been lucky that the shock he had felt on seeing her face on the flyers hadn't given him away.

He had managed to grab the flyers and had then gone back and torn down every one of them that he could find posted along Duval street. Of course, that was just a short-term answer. He was sure that they would go back up again the next day. And if he removed them a second time, somebody might wonder why.

He headed back to the house. It wouldn't due to leave Georgie alone with her for too long. He didn't trust his little brother because he wasn't quite right in the head. But he had always taken care of him after their parents had died. Unlike some people, he didn't think of Georgie as a burden. Georgie listened to him and he did what he was told. But sometimes Georgie didn't always listen and when that happened, he fucked things up and he had to straighten Georgie out.

Storms made Georgie nervous, so he needed to get home to him. The roar of the thunder and the rain beating on the windows had scared Georgie during the hurricane. When Georgie got scared was when he didn't follow instructions. He pulled into the driveway and headed for the front door. Moments later he was inside, and Georgie emerged from the back of the house.

"What were you doing back there, Georgie? Were you bothering the girl?" he demanded.

"No, Oscar. You told me to stay out of the room if you weren't here. So, that is what I did. I just went to the door because of the storm. I was scared."

"But you didn't go inside the room?"

"No, because you told me not to."

Chapter Three

His head didn't hurt as bad when he woke up. That was a good thing. Marlow slowly stood and headed for the bathroom. He took care of business and then stepped in the shower. A quick shampoo removed the dried blood from his scalp and set his head to aching again. Toweling himself dry, he swallowed two aspirin dry. Cinching the towel around his waist, Marlow padded out to the kitchen and started a pot of coffee.

He was still trying to sort out what had happened the night before. He had been ambushed all right, but why? Had it been because of the flyers? It seemed a good bet since they were the only thing that was taken. His revolver and his wallet were left untouched, which was pretty strange for an ordinary mugging. Why mug him if not for valuables? Marlow pondered that as he padded back to the bedroom and removed a fresh pair of cargo shorts, underwear, socks and undershirt from the drawer of clothes that he kept in Tina's apartment. He got dressed, threaded his belt through the loops on the shorts and clipped his holster onto his belt. He snared a green Aloha Shirt from a hanger in the closet and pulled it on and went back to the kitchen and poured a cup of coffee. He added a packet of sweetener and stirred it in before taking a sip. Finally, he picked up his cell phone and dialed Jamie Gutierrez.

"What's up Rick?" Gutierrez asked, sounding very businesslike.

"Any chance you can meet me at 'Harpoon Harry's' for breakfast? My treat?" Marlow asked.

"Hell. Yes, if you're buying!"

"Meet you there in about fifteen minutes," Marlow said before breaking the connection. He stuffed his cell phone into his pocket and headed for the door. Marlow locked it on his way out. He wanted to pick up his car before heading over to 'Harpoon Harry's' to eat.

Marlow was just crossing the street when he spotted the chief of police walking up from the other direction. "Morning, Chief," he greeted him.

"Marlow, to what do I owe the pleasure?" Gutierrez asked, as they stepped through the door.

"Hey, guys. Table or booth?" Ron asked. He was the owner.

"Table in the back if you have one open," Marlow spoke first.

"Sure thing," Ron said, as he turned and waved one of the waitresses to them. "Cathy, take them to the table in the back corner."

"Follow me, please. My name is Cathy and I'll be your server today," she said leading them to the back. She knew them both since they were regulars, but she pretended it was their first time in. Once they were seated, she handed them menus and quickly disappeared back to the front.

"Why am I here, Rick?" Gutierrez asked.

"I have a new case. A girl came here and disappeared

during Irma," Marlow explained.

"A lot of people disappeared before and during Irma, Marlow."

"Well, this girl's mother hired me to find out what happened to her. I was putting up flyers last night on Duval and I got mugged during the storm. The only thing that the mugger took was the stack of flyers that I hadn't put up yet."

"That does seem pretty strange. It almost has to be related."

"I agree. That's why I wanted to pick your brain to see what you thought about it.

"My first guess is that somebody has her and doesn't want people to know about it."

"That was my thought, as well. If I print up some more and bring them to the station will you have them passed out to all of the officers so that they can be on the lookout for her?"

"I can do that," Jamie nodded. Cathy returned to take their orders. Both ordered *café con leche's,* a sugary Cuban coffee drink that was very popular in South Florida. They, also, ordered eggs over easy, hash browns, and toast, as well as, a couple of slices of bacon. Cathy headed away with their order.

"I'll bring them to your office in a couple of hours," Marlow said, taking a sip of his ice water.

"This case worries you," Gutierrez observed.

"It does. Quinn Kerns was only sixteen years old. She was being molested at home by her father. So, she ran hoping to find a new start. Now, she may well be involved in worse treatment than what she had run away from to begin with."

"You want to find her and give her a choice, don't you?"

"I do. I think that if I find her alive, she deserves that. Don't you?"

"I do. Bring me the flyers and I'll have officers keep an eye out," Jamie replied. Cathy reappeared with their meals. She placed them in front of them and quickly disappeared. Both men dug into their meals, foregoing their discussion until the food was gone.

"I really am trying to stay off of your toes, Jamie. I know the council has come down hard on you over your involvement in 'The Hemingway Case,'" Marlow said.

"Not as much as they could have. They are very protective of the Hemingway legacy here on the island. The fact that the manuscript was found has kept a certain amount of heat off of me. Especially, since it was destroyed so that it couldn't become a governmental embarrassment."

"Thank Harry Dove for that. He could have blown the whistle, but he didn't," Marlow told him.

"I know that. Harry has been a pain in my ass, but he has also been a useful one," Gutierrez agreed.

"Yeah, I heard about 'The Sunset Strangler Case'. If it wasn't for Harry, you might never had ended his spree," Marlow nodded.

"I know that, too," Jamie sighed.

"You want another *café con leche?*" Marlow asked.

"No, I'm good," the chief of police said, standing and heading for the front of the restaurant. Marlow waited on Cathy to come back and ordered another to go. He paid the check, left a good size tip and walked out with his second *café con leche* and headed for his car.

Marlow got in and started the car, kicking the AC on

high. It was nine a.m. and the temperature was already in the low nineties. He headed for the office. He wanted to talk to Walter about the events of the night before. Marlow hoped that the wily old attorney might have some ideas about why Marlow had been attacked and the flyers stolen.

The only thing that Marlow could think of was that the girl was still alive, and somebody didn't want her found. The big question for him was why? What could be the purpose for keeping her alive? He wished Tina were here instead of Chicago. She had a good head for figuring things out and he had come to rely on her for her insights.

He pulled into Walter's driveway and parked. He got out, locking the doors and entered through his office. Marlow sat down and turned on his computer. As it booted up, he opened the door to the hallway and walked to the conference room. He could see Lola Ponsberry already at the reception desk. That meant Walter was already in the conference room. So, that was where Marlow headed.

Walter Loomis was seated behind the large maple table, stacks of folders on each side of him. Some were open cases, some were cases that he was reviewing. Marlow walked in and dropped into the seat across from him.

"Ricky, what may I do for you?" Walter asked.

"The search for Quinn Kerns. There had been some developments," Marlow told him.

"Developments? Explain, please," Walter said, his gaze sharpening.

"I was posting flyers along Duval. A storm hit, and as I was heading for Tina's place, I got mugged. The only thing they took was the flyers," Marlow explained.

"That does seem odd," Walter nodded.

31

"I thought so, too."

"So, what do you think is behind it?"

"I'm not sure. The person that took her, he took her for a reason. What that reason was, I have no idea," Marlow explained.

"And you think I might?" Walter looked at him.

"I was hoping," Marlow admitted.

"I am sad to say that it was a forlorn hope, at best, Ricky. I'm sure I have no idea," Walter told him.

"It was worth a shot, Walter," Marlow shrugged.

"I'm sure it was."

"So, what are you going to do about it?"

"I'm going to hunt for the person that took her."

"You believe that you can find her?"

"I do."

"I pray that you're right, Ricky."

"Me too," Marlow told him.

Marlow headed back to his office to make up more flyers. He would cover the ground again, but this time he would do it in daylight. He would also get some to the Key West Police Department since Jamie had promised to have his officers keep an eye out for Quinn. Except, Marlow didn't really hold much hope that the police would be able to find her. They had too much to do in the aftermath of Irma to concentrate their time and energy to searching for one missing teenager.

So, it would come down to Marlow and what he could do. He pulled up the file and printed off more flyers. His first stop would be the police station, and then he would start putting them up all over the island. He also emailed a copy of the flyer to the sheriff's department and to the

Florida Department of Law Enforcement.

~ ~ ~

Chief Jamie Gutierrez leaned back in his chair. He was fully recovered from his gunshot wound and had fully resumed his duties as the head of the Key West Police Department. His men had been working overtime ever since the hurricane. Crime didn't take a vacation and even a hurricane couldn't stop it. But, he kept coming back to what Marlow had told him about the girl vanishing.

It didn't set well with him. Not at all. He didn't like people vanishing on his island. Marlow was going to be surprised, because he was going to have extra help looking for Quinn Kerns.

~ ~ ~

Marlow walked into the police station with a stack of flyers under his arm. He asked for the chief and was immediately buzzed through. Jamie met him half way to his office. "Those the flyers?" he asked, holding his hand out. Marlow passed them to him.

"They are," Marlow replied.

"I'll make sure that they go out with every officer in every car. Bicycle patrol will have them, too," Gutierrez told him.

"I appreciate that, Jamie."

"It is what friends are for, amigo. I don't like people disappearing off my island on my watch."

"Thank you. I'll call if I find anything."

"Same here," the chief told him. Marlow nodded and headed back outside to his car. He would park in the city lot and then go up and down Duval putting up flyers. Then, he would put them up all over the rest of the island and across the bridge on Stock Island, as well. Somebody had to have seen Quinn after she had arrived on Key West.

All Marlow needed to do was find them. It sounded simple when he put it like that, but it was anything but. Key West was a tourist town, and as such, it had a very transient population. That was both a strength and a weakness when it came to trying to find a missing person.

People knew that Quinn arrived might well have left the island before Irma struck. There was a chance that they might not come back, which wouldn't help him at all. No, he needed to find someone that knew her before the storm and that had stayed. That was going to be tough, but he would find a way. There were some of the street kids he knew that would be willing to help because he had helped them out in the past.

Marlow headed to Smathers Beach. Rocco Habanera would be there. Rocco was one of the many homeless teens that called the rock their home. Plus, Rocco owed Marlow a favor for keeping him from getting busted for vagrancy.

Rocco was a white kid with a deep Bronx accent and dark hair. The kid was an expert windsurfer and he knew all of the kids that were looking for places to stay. If anybody would know Quinn, it would be Rocco.

Despite the ongoing cleanup, the wind surfers were out on the water. It was just a matter of time until Rocco came in. Marlow planned to be there when he did.

Of course, Rocco was only his first stop among the homeless teens that called Key West home. Marlow knew that he would find others. One of them surely, would have met Quinn Kerns.

Chapter Four

Marlow climbed out of his car and walked down the path to the sand. A lot of the locals had come to the beach to take a break from the cleanup. Marlow carried a handheld cooler he had filled up with ice and Killian's Red and walked to a likely spot where he could see the windsurfers riding the breeze over the water, their boards cutting through the small waves. He sat down and opened the cooler, pulled out a chilled bottle and twisted off the cap, dropping it into his shirt pocket. The cold beer tasted good going down.

It didn't take long for him to spot Rocco out there on his board. The kid was one of the best. He worked part time at one of the shops on the island that catered to the windsurfing crowd and lived with a bunch of other kids that they all pitched in for rent. Marlow had met him when he was busting up a pickpocket ring that was working Duval Street and Mallory Square on the weekends.

Rocco had proved to be a valuable source of information ever since. He had helped Marlow cultivate other kids to help him out with an informal network of what Walter sometimes referred to as his 'Baker Street Irregulars' referencing a Sherlock Holmes tale.

Marlow drained his first beer and pulled out a second.

It was damned hot on the beach. Finally, Rocco headed for shore. He began taking down the sail to stow it as Marlow finished his second beer. Marlow stood, grabbed the cooler and walked over to him.

"Rocco. You looked good out there," Marlow told the teen.

"Marlow? What can I do for you, brah?" Rocco asked, sticking his hand out to shake. Marlow took it and shook the boy's hand.

"I'm looking for a girl, Rocco. She would have hit town before the storm. Nobody has seen her since," Marlow explained, pulling out a flyer and handing it over. Rocco unfolded it and looked at the picture.

"She looks familiar, but I can't be sure," Rocco said, after studying the picture.

"Can you show these around? See if anybody met her?"

"I sure can."

"I'm willing to pay for information. Make sure everybody knows that. But it has to pan out before I pay."

"Don't worry, boss. I'll put the word out and I'll make sure everybody understands."

"Thanks, Rocco. I'm really worried about this girl," Marlow told him.

Marlow headed back to his car. There were still other places and people he needed to see. After that, he was going to head over to Stock Island and look around over there.

~ ~ ~

Marlow found Thom Hark in the 'Chart Room' having lunch. The lunch crowd was a lot lighter than normal but that suited Marlow just fine. Thom was seated in his usual spot and he waved Marlow over when he saw him. "Ricky, so good to see you," Thom said, as Marlow dropped into the seat across from him. "I take it you weathered the storm okay?"

"I did. How about you and your lovely wife?" Marlow asked in response.

"We made it through and with little damage. We were luckier than some," Thom admitted.

"I'm glad to hear it, Thom. I've been helping with clean up all over the island."

"So, I hear. Jack Marsh had mentioned you helping him. Finn Pilar noted your help with the cleanup, also."

"Why is that such a big deal?" Marlow asked in exasperation.

"It's a story because you aren't a true Conch, but you are now being accepted as such. That's a good thing, Rick, if you believe it or not. It is actually helping your growing reputation on the island," Hark explained.

"If it helps me find this missing girl, then I am all for it," Marlow replied.

"So, tell me about her," Thom prompted.

"Right," Marlow said. "Her name is Quinn Kerns, she arrived a week before Irma hit."

"And then?"

"Nobody has seen her since."

"That is not good, not good at all."

"That's the way I see it as well."

"You know I'll help by publishing a story in the Citizen, along with her picture," Thom told him.

"You might mention that there is a five-hundred-dollar reward for information that leads to finding her, payable when she is found," Marlow added.

"That should get people to open their eyes and look around," Thom nodded.

"I wish I had time to join you for lunch, but I still have people to see."

"Have you checked with the cab drivers? They see a lot of people."

"Another good idea, Thom. Have you ever thought about changing professions?" Marlow asked with a grin.

"Your work is far too strenuous for a man of my years, Ricky. I'll stick to reporting the news," Thom Hark replied.

"Which reminds me, have you seen Harry Dove around lately?"

"Afraid not. Last I heard, he was up in Miami chasing down some story about someone using alligators to murder people along the Tamiami Trail."

"Harry does like the strange cases."

"Oh, he lives for them," Thom nodded as Marlow stood and headed for the door. Thom shook his head and took a long pull on his beer. He hoped that Marlow found the girl and that she was well.

~ ~ ~

Marlow had the AC running as he pulled out from the 'Pier House Resort' parking lot. The temperature was soaring as the sun rose higher into the morning sky. On impulse, he headed home and traded his car for the ancient yellow Huffy ten speed that had been his main transportation for the first couple of years after his Ford Pinto had been blown up during his first case working for Walter Loomis.

Marlow peddled towards Old Town, wanting to check on some things. First, he wanted to see if any of the flyers he had posted the day before were still up. He had a gut feeling that they would be gone. Especially, after what had happened last night.

Marlow was sweating by the time he reached Duval Street. He rode his bike to Mallory Square and locked it in a rack and then started back down Duval, tracing his steps from the night before. None of the flyers remained. They had all been torn down. So, Marlow stopped and hung up new ones, and went into shops to hand them to employees so they could keep an eye out, as well.

The thing about trying to find someone that was missing was a bit like looking for a needle in a haystack. Luck played into it as much as anything. He would just have to swim through the haystack and hoped he got stung by the needle. Not the greatest of plans, but it was what he had to work with.

It was damned little. He wished that Tina would call him. She was very good for bouncing theories off of. She had a unique insight into people and their motives from her work as a server.

~ ~ ~

Steve Lorca put his chainsaw down and wiped the sweat from his brow. He had started early this morning, helping cut away downed trees and branches. He wanted to get the island up and running as soon as possible. Key West was a tourist town, and they needed tourism to stay profitable. Still, his mind was troubled.

~ ~ ~

Georgie stretched as he got out of bed. He knew that Oscar had gone to work. Georgie wanted to look at the girl. She was so pretty. Oscar had given him her clothes to wash

39

and dry. But Georgie hadn't washed her panties. Nope indeed! He had kept them hidden in his pillow and he put them to his face at night smelled the crotch of them. He had even licked them a few times and imagined that he could taste her. She wasn't the first one that he had kept their panties. He had three different pairs. He would give her a clean pair with her clothes. When he put the clothes in her room, he would look at her thin body and imagine what it would be like to have her when she wasn't unconscious. Oscar said that Georgie got too excited when the girls were awake and that he scared them. But he didn't think that Oscar was telling the truth about that.

No, Georgie didn't believe that he scared the girls near as much as Oscar did. Oscar could be very scary when he got angry. Sometimes, he hurt Georgie when he got mad. Afterwards, he said he hadn't meant too, but Georgie was pretty sure that Oscar lied about that too.

~ ~ ~

Kieran Snow was standing and looking at some of the flyers that had gone up on corkboards at several establishments in Old Town. She looked for help wanted ads. She was able to find enough day jobs to keep her in cash, so she could pay the rent on her little studio apartment. Then she saw a flyer about a missing girl. Kieran moved closer to study the picture.

It took her a minute, but she recognized the girl. Her name was Quinn. She had met her not long after the girl had gotten off the bus in Key West.

Quinn had come down from Miami, a haunted look in her eye. It was a look that Kieran recognized because she had seen that same look in her own eyes when she left home after her father had molested her. She had taken Quinn in, helped her get settled. Then, the day before the storm hit, Quinn hadn't come back to the apartment.

Kieran had thought that Quinn had just taken a bus and evacuated like many other residents had done with Hurricane Irma bearing down on the Keys. She hadn't thought much about it when Quinn hadn't come back afterwards, figuring that the girl had either gone home or had gone somewhere else.

But now, with seeing the missing flyer, she suddenly felt sick. Because she knew that she should have tried harder to find Quinn. There was a phone number on the bottom of the flyer. Kieran tore one of them off and tucked it into the pocket of her shorts. She would call it later when she got time. She owed Quinn that much!

~ ~ ~

Marlow had finished reposting the flyers, as well as dropping a number of them off at both the police and fire departments. The mugging the night before was still bothering him. Somebody didn't want Quinn Kerns found. He had to wonder why.

Was it because that she had seen something that she should not have? Or was it something worse? There was no way to know. He shook his head.

Marlow headed back towards 'Harpoon Harry's'. He was ready for lunch and the restaurant was close. When Tina wasn't working, he didn't go to 'Pepe's'. It just made him miss her all the more.

It was Monday. So, he ordered the baked meatloaf and mashed potatoes and gravy. It was the best meal on the island for ten bucks or less. Teresa brought him his plate and a cup of coffee. Marlow devoured it quickly and paid the check before heading back outside. He was glad to know that Ron had replaced the windows with bulletproof glass, after all the times that Mad Mick Murphy had got the place shot up.

The sun was overhead and hot when Marlow had finished his meal. He hopped on his Huffy and headed back to his house to pick up the car. He would drive it back to the office where it would be handy if he figured out any new avenue of investigation.

~ ~ ~

Oscar James frowned as he looked around Duval Street. The flyers had gone back up, but there was little he could do about it now. He had to maintain his cover. Nobody knew his real name or who he really was. That worked in his favor. He would use it as long as he could.

One thing he was sure of. Rick Marlow had to die. Because if Marlow were to expose him, Oscar knew that he would be the one to die.

He had to stop Marlow, one way or another! There was no question about that.

~ ~ ~

Marlow had locked his bike up before getting into his Ford Escort and putting it in gear. The AC had the car very cool by the time he pulled into Walter's driveway.

Chapter Five

Marlow locked his car before unlocking the door to his office and stepping inside. The air conditioning was a welcome relief after the blistering heat outside. Marlow grabbed his coffee cup and poured some of the still warm brew into it before heading down the hall to talk to Walter. His boss had a lot of insight into how things worked on the island, and he might well know a few other people that Marlow could enlist in the search.

The door to the conference room opened and a lady stepped out. She was tall and willowy with long dark hair that was braided into a long French braid the almost reached her waist. She wore a white silk dress that clung to her in all the right spots. She offered him a smile before heading for the front door. Marlow paused to admire her retreating form. He spotted Lola watching him and rolling her eyes.

Marlow gave her a smile and walked into the conference room. Walter sat behind the table like a benign Buddha, holding court over numerous files and a yellow legal pad of which he was folding over the page when Marlow entered.

"Ricky, what is on your mind?" Walter asked, his eyes somewhat owlish behind the thick lenses of his glasses.

"The police department and the sheriff's office have copies of the flyers. I rehung them all over town again after someone tore them all down last night. I've also talked to the head of my 'Baker Street Irregulars' as you call them, and he is spreading the word among the teens and homeless on the island as well," Marlow replied.

"So, what is your next step?"

"I was wondering if you had any ideas. Thom is also going to put her picture and story in The Citizen."

"It sounds like you have certainly covered all of your bases."

"Perhaps, but it just feels like I am missing something."

"You've missed nothing that I can see, Ricky."

Marlow took a sip of his coffee. "My mind keeps going back to my mugging last night. Whoever did it took the flyers I had left. Why would they do that unless they didn't want anybody looking for Quinn Kerns."

"That seems like an appropriate theory."

"It does. But it also makes me wonder why they don't want anybody looking for her."

"That is the question isn't it? Have looked to see if there have been any other unusual disappearances? Going back even before the storm?" Walter asked.

"That's a very good idea. I'll do a computer search first and see what I can find. Then, I'll ask Jamie to check the missing person's reports. You might just be on to something, Walter," Marlow told the older man.

"I pray that I'm wrong, Ricky. Because if I'm not, it means that we have a serial killer here on the island," Walter sighed.

"I hope you are wrong too, old friend," Marlow told

44

him. He picked up his coffee cup and headed back down the hall to his office.

The idea of a serial kidnapper and or killer terrified him on a very deep level. Key West depended on tourism. If word got out that there was serial killer was on the rock, tourism would die until the guy was caught or killed. The island couldn't afford that. Not after the destruction that Irma had wrought on the Keys.

~ ~ ~

Keiran Snow finished up the house cleaning job and had gotten paid. Now she was back out on the street. She had just reached Duval Street and spotted another one of the flyers with Quinn Kerns' picture on it. It reminded her of the number she had torn off one of the flyers earlier. She pulled the number and her cell phone out and dialed the number on it.

~ ~ ~

Marlow got to his office just as the telephone started ringing. He scooped it up. "Marlow, how can I help you?" he asked.

"Are you the guy looking for Quinn?" asked a young female voice.

"I am. Have you seen her?" he asked.

"She was living with me, and then . . . she didn't come home the night before the hurricane hit. I just figured she had caught a ride back to Miami, ya' know?"

"I can understand. Except she never went back."

"Oh, my God! Can you find her?" Kieran asked.

"I'm going to try. May I have your name?" Marlow asked politely.

"Kieran, Kieran Snow. I should have called the police

when she didn't come back."

"You had no way to know, Kieran. Do you know if she had any other friends?"

"Not that I know of. I met her right after she got off the bus from Miami. She didn't know anybody here. She ran away from home because her father was molesting her," Kieran said softly.

"I know about that, too. Think back, Kieran, did she mention anyone else that she had met?"

"There was some guy she met at Mallory Square one night, but she never mentioned his name."

"You did the right thing to call me. This information is some I didn't have before," Marlow told her.

"Will you be able to find her and make sure that she is okay?" Kieran asked softly.

"I'll do my best, Kieran. That's all I can promise," Marlow replied.

"Thank you," Kieran said before hanging up. Marlow leaned back in his chair. Mallory Square was packed every night by locals and tourists waiting to watch the most beautiful sunset in the world and hoping to see the legendary green flash in the sky that signaled good luck for those that saw it.

If Walter's theory was right and there was another serial killer on Key West, then he had a wealth of possible targets that would never be missed, at least not locally. Marlow reached for the telephone and dialed Thom Hark.

"Hark," Thom answered the telephone.

"Thom, this is Marlow. Can you give me a rundown on every missing person's case filed in the last six months?"

"It might take me a while, but I think I can scan the

police reports and find the information that you are looking for," Thom said.

"Thank you, Thom, I appreciate this," Marlow told him.

"Call me back in a couple of hours," Thom told him. Marlow hung up the telephone. The sun was starting to go down. Marlow went outside and unlocked the cable holding his bike to the rack and then peddled his way to Mallory Square. Maybe there, he could find the boy that Quinn had met. It was worth a shot at least.

~ ~ ~

Marlow walked into the burgeoning crowd that filled Mallory Square on a nightly basis to watch the sunset. He was looking for a positive suspect, and hoped that he might find one, albeit a drunk witness. So far, he had no luck.

He was getting a bad feeling about this case and about Quinn Kerns. Somebody didn't want her found. That frightened him a little because it made him think that she might already be dead. Or that his poking around might make whoever had her decide to get rid of her sooner than later. He wished he could talk to Tina. She saw things in ways that he couldn't and often could give him insights into things that he would never have considered.

He moved to an area that was relatively quiet and uncrowded and pulled out his Windows phone. He checked the time. Tina would be done with court for the day. He pulled up his speed dial and called her. She answered on the second ring.

"What's up, Ricky?" Tina's voice filled his ear.

"Just wanted to check in and see how things are going for you back in Chicago," Marlow told her.

"So far, so good. I should be able to come back home

soon," Tina said wistfully.

"I hope so, I miss you," Marlow told her.

"I know you do," Tina replied, and he could feel her smile.

"I'll make sure to order in a great welcome home meal," Marlow told her.

"Why not cook one?"

"You have tasted my cooking, right? The only things I make well are chili and spaghetti."

"You, also, bake a good garlic bread. So, how about spaghetti and garlic bread for my welcome home meal? Add in some pinot grigio to drink?" Tina asked.

"Let me know your flight time and I'll have it ready before I leave to pick you up."

"You've got a deal. I'll call you when I have a flight time," Tina told him before hanging up. Marlow was grinning, as he slipped his phone back into the pocket of his shorts. Marlow was whistling a happy tune as he made his way back into the throngs of tourist ready to watch the sunset.

Chapter Six

Marlow had just hung up when something hit him and sent him stumbling towards the edge of the seawall. He was trying catch his balance and turn when he was hit again, his legs catching the concrete ledge before he fell into space and made the short drop into the ocean. Luckily, he had been able to take a breath before hitting the water and he quickly pushed back to the surface. Already quick minded tourists were leaning over the edging and extending hands down to him to help pull him out of the water.

Once back on solid ground, the adrenaline spike had started to wear off. Soaked to the skin and dripping salt water, Marlow headed for Tina's place, so he could change clothes and clean his revolver before the sea water started corroding it. Somebody had gotten close enough to him to shove him off Sunset Pier. He had forgotten the first rule of being a cop. Keep your head on a swivel and be aware of your surroundings at all times. And it had almost gotten him killed. He couldn't afford to be that careless again.

Marlow made it to Tina's apartment without further mishap. He unlocked the door, stepped inside, took off his shoes and stripped to the skin. He carried his revolver in his right hand and his wet clothes in his left as he headed to the small laundry room.

Marlow hadn't turned on any lights. He knew where everything in the apartment was and could easily navigate in the darkness. He had just stepped on the cool tile of the kitchen floor when he realized that he was not alone in the apartment. He could vaguely make out a shape heading for the door he had just entered the apartment.

It was too dark to make out who it was, and the only thing he could tell was that it was a white male. He lifted his revolver and hoped that it would still fire after being immersed in sea water. "Stop right there!" Marlow commanded. There was a flash of light and thunder of sound. Marlow dived for cover, triggering his own revolver. He heard a muffled curse and then the front door opened and closed. Marlow pushed to his feet and ran for the door. He threw it open and stepped partially outside, looking in both directions. Whoever it had been, they were long gone. He looked down and saw blood drops on the sidewalk.

However, he was stark naked and in no condition to follow the blood trail. Marlow stepped back inside and locked the door. This time he turned on the lights as he made his way through the apartment and recovered his wet clothing. He put them in the washer, added soap and a plastic ball of fabric softener and started the clothes washing. He grabbed a fluffy white terrycloth house robe from the bathroom and dialed the police station. "May I speak to Chief Gutierrez?" Marlow asked when he got an answer.

"Let me see if he is still here," The operator told him. Marlow waited patiently as a Jimmy Buffet tune filled the empty space.

"Hello?" Jamie's voice sounded in his ear a moment later.

"I need to report a break in and two attempts on my life," Marlow told him.

"Where are you?" Gutierrez asked.

"I'm at Tina's place."

"I'll be there in five," Gutierrez told him, hanging up the phone. The washer was still at work when the chief knocked on the door and Marlow answered it. He had been in the process of cleaning his revolver with a kit that he kept at Tina's house. He had a Phoenix Arms .22 in his robe pocket when he went to answer the door.

"What the hell is going on, Marlow?" Gutierrez asked as he stepped inside.

"Somebody knocked me off the pier tonight, and when I got back here, there was somebody here tossing Tina's apartment. They took a shot at me and I shot back, but they got away. They left a blood trail outside, but since I was naked I didn't choose to follow it. I figured that was best left to professionals like yourself," Marlow replied.

"Where's Tina?" Gutierrez asked.

"With luck, she is currently on a plane heading home. She was in Chicago testifying against the twin of that guy that had stalked her[3]." Marlow explained.

"I remember that. She flying into Miami?" Jamie asked.

"I think so."

"So, what do you think the guy that had broken in was after?"

"I wish I knew," Marlow replied honestly.

~ ~ ~

It had been a close thing, him getting close enough to

---

[3] Marlow: Something wicked

dump Marlow over the side of the Sunset Pier. He hadn't counted on him getting to Tina's place as quickly as he had. He was paying for that with a shoulder wound and blood staining his shirt as he headed back home. He would get his little brother to remove the bullet and bandage the wound.

That was one more thing that Marlow would have to pay for. One of many things since this whole affair had started. He could not allow anybody to find out about Quinn. Not until he was done with her at least.

~ ~ ~

Tina Cord frowned as her plane lifted into the air. She had been lucky enough to get a seat because a passenger had not shown up on time. She was worried about Ricky. He had sounded so fragile when she had spoken to him. Something was wrong, and she was sure that it had nothing to do with him missing her.

Had she been targeted somehow by one of his many enemies? There was no real way to tell. All she could do was be aware of her surroundings and keep an eye out for anything that was out of the ordinary.

Ricky had taught her that much. Maybe it was time for putting his lessons into practice!

~ ~ ~

After locking the apartment up tight, Marlow had showered and cleaned his gun. He had washed his clothes and put them into the dryer. He needed to go home and feed and water Misty. The little gray cat had filled as much of the hole in his heart, and Tina had filled the rest. He walked out to the parking lot where he had left his car. He climbed in and headed back to his duplex.

There was some weird shit going on with this case. What made Quinn Kerns so special to the abductor? Because Marlow was sure that she had been abducted and had not took a bus back to the mainland to avoid Irma. If she had, somebody would have heard from her by now.

No, somebody had her hidden on the island. His gut was rarely wrong. Right now, he needed to swap out his revolver for another gun and move his sim card to his backup phone and hoped that the sea water hadn't scrambled it. He would put the wet phone into a bag of rice to try and dry it out.

It was clear that whoever had Quinn had started stalking him to try and make sure that he didn't find her. That meant that whoever it was, wanted to keep her and continue to torture her. Which in turn, meant that she was still alive.

Misty the cat jumped off the couch and ran to him when he entered the apartment. Marlow reached down and scooped her up, holding her and scratching under her chin and on the sides of her face as she purred loudly. He carried her to his bedroom and gently set her on the bed before sitting down himself.

He pulled open the drawer on the nightstand and pulled out his Ruger 9mm SCP. He popped the magazine, checked the load and then slapped it back into the butt of the pistol to make sure that it seated properly. He worked the slide to chamber the top round off the magazine and slipped it into the pocket holster that went into his right-hand pocket. He then pulled the back off his old phone and took out the sim. He opened his back up and slid the sim card in to place and put the back in place and turned the cell phone on. He carried the pieces of the old phone back to the kitchen and put them in a plastic bag and filled it with rice. He would check it in the morning.

The killer was out there in the night somewhere. Marlow meant to find him before he could kill again.

He gave Misty a quick pat on the head and headed for the kitchen. She followed, giving him a questioning look. Marlow filled her dish with kitty food and made sure her water dish was full.

"I'll be home later," He told her as she attacked the food.

Marlow headed for the door. He needed to head back to Duval Street to see if he might have any luck finding who had pushed him off the pier. More than likely, whoever had done it was long gone. He had decided to take his ten speed this time. It would be easier to find parking for the bike than it would for the Ford.

~ ~ ~

Jamie Gutierrez had followed the blood trail until it stopped at the far end of the parking lot. The intruder had gotten away. He would contact the hospitals and let them know to be on the lookout for a gunshot wound. Other than that, there was not much he could do.

He was worried about Marlow and this case. He was worried about Tina as well. The storm, Irma, had decimated the Florida Keys. They would be working until spring before they made a full recovery. Marlow was not himself when Tina was gone. She completed him in ways that Marlow himself didn't realize.

Jamie knew the feeling well. He had suffered through it after breaking things off with Elise. Elise and her uncle had managed to keep 'Midnight Blues' open even after he had withdrawn his financial support. But it had been a near thing.

He avoided the club and Elise as much as possible, but he still missed both. Jamie loved jazz, and he loved the sound of Elise's voice as she sang old jazz standards. There was a strange feel to the island, like perhaps the Haitian Vodou Baron Samedi had returned to wreak havoc on the island once more! He had felt it had happened before when the club had first opened.

~ ~ ~

Duval Street was crowded and full of celebration of life as the witching hour approached. Marlow walked the street up and down, searching for anyone that might possibly have any information about Quinn Kerns.

This time, however, Marlow was doing it right. His eyes never stopped moving as he surveyed the crowd while walking Duval. He saw a few people stop to look at the flyers, but they didn't look long and none of them appeared to recognize the young girl's face. That was a disappointment, but one that he had actually expected.

He hadn't heard back from Rocco yet, but that was to be expected. The homeless kids and drifters had their own version of the coconut telegraph, sometimes it was faster, sometimes, it was slower. According to Kieran Snow, Quinn had met a guy at Mallory Square and had gotten to know him. Could the guy she met have taken her? He needed to find out who that guy was.

Mallory Square would be mostly deserted at this hour, but he headed there anyway. A breeze was blowing in off the water and it felt good, even if it was still a warm breeze after dark. The wind ruffled his hair. It reached almost to the top of his shoulders, and Tina liked it longer. Marlow wondered if he was still being followed. If so, the empty square might be a good place to confront the son of a bitch!

~ ~ ~

He had been surprised to see Marlow back out on the street after their earlier meeting in Tina Cord's apartment. His simpleminded brother had dug out the bullet in his shoulder and had sewn up the wound. Antibiotic cream had been slathered over it before the heavy gauze pad and bandage had been taped in place over the wound. He had on a wife beater tank shirt on under an oversized Aloha shirt so that the bandage wasn't noticeable. He knew that he was pushing himself to the limit, maybe even beyond his own level of endurance, but he wasn't finished with Quinn yet. He wanted to take his time with her. She was special. He had seen that when he had first met her on Mallory Square.

He remembered how she had looked. Her long hair blowing in the breeze. Her skin was tanned, and her legs were long in a pair of short shorts and sandals. She had been wearing a blue denim sleeveless shirt with a ruffle of the same material on it. Her eyes were a brilliant blue that made him feel like he was falling into them.

~ ~ ~

Marlow strolled out onto the brick covered pier. Shadows were thick, and he made sure to move into them and keep to them, vanishing into the darkness. He spotted a man that had been trailing him at a distance, but the guy was too far away for him to see his face. His shape looked familiar but was too far away for him to make anything out.

But the guy stopped when he couldn't spot Marlow. The guy stood there for a couple of moments and then turned and headed back for Duval. But this time, Marlow was on his trail.

Chapter Seven

It was nearing midnight as Marlow followed his mystery tail back onto Duval Street. The streets were crowded as usual for the time. Neon lights blazed, and music blared from the many bars. Party goers laughed and sang along as they moved along the streets. Taxis dropped off and picked up, the only effect was the changes in faces on the street. The police were around, both in cars and on bicycles, to keep order.

Marlow stayed about half a block back, keeping his eyes on the white ball cap that the man was wearing, the bill shadowing his face. There was something familiar in the way that he moved, but Marlow couldn't place him. That aggravated the crap out of him, which is why he was caught by surprise when a party surged out of one of the bars and sent him stumbling into the street and into the path of an oncoming car. It stopped with a screech of brakes, but not before Marlow bounced off the hood and onto the pavement. Cursing, he pushed his way to his feet and looked for the man he had been tailing. The guy was gone, vanished without a trace.

Marlow was rubbing his thigh where the car had hit him when a police officer arrived on the scene. Marlow told the cop he didn't need an ambulance and started back to where he had left his car parked, frustrated and angry that he had lost the first lead he had been able to dig up on the missing girl.

~ ~ ~

Misty, the cat, was waiting on him when he returned home. She rubbed against his legs purring loudly and he bent and picked her up, cuddling her against his chest as he walked to the kitchen after locking his door. She was rubbing her head against the bottom of his chin, her long hair soft and comforting as he got out a glass and filled it with vodka and diet cranberry pineapple juice. He carried Misty and his drink back to the living room and sat down on the beat-up couch. He turned on the TV and found and old movie starting Bogart and Bacall in 'Dark Passage' playing on one of the cable stations out of Miami. He petted the cat and emptied the tall glass before drifting off to sleep.

~ ~ ~

He was shocked at how careless he had gotten. If it hadn't been for Marlow getting shoved out into traffic, he might have led the private eye right back to his home and the girl, and that was something that he could not do. He wanted time to play more with Quinn, to let her experience every sort of depravity that could be inflicted on her. When he was done and had dumped her, maybe her fate would deter other young women from flocking to Key West to flaunt their moral ambiguity! The island had been a nice place to live once, back before it had become a tourist destination. Now, most of the women that came to the island came to put their sexuality on display, to flaunt their bodies and seek unlimited sexual conquests. The girls were actually worse than the multitudes of young men who came searching to get laid at the 'End of the Road.'

They teased people like his simpleminded brother, lured him with their sex and then laughed at him and made fun of him for his lack of understanding of what was being done to him. His brother had suffered greatly at their hands. But that didn't happen anymore.

~ ~ ~

Morning arrived with somebody pounding on his door. Marlow opened his eyes and noticed that Misty was curled up asleep in his lap. He gently moved her over to one of the cushions without waking her and made his way to the offending door. He peered through the peephole, surprised to see Chief Gutierrez standing on the other side.

Marlow opened the door and let him inside. "You look like shit, Marlow," Chief Gutierrez observed.

"Yeah, well, yesterday was a rough day," Marlow shrugged.

"Tina not back yet?"

"Not yet, but I do expect her soon."

"She's good for you Marlow. Don't let her get away."

"I don't plan on it," Marlow replied, wishing he had a cigarette. He had successfully managed to quite a couple of years back, but he still had the craving. He wasn't sure that would ever go away.

"You need a little hair of the dog?" Jamie asked.

"Nope, just a shower and some breakfast."

"I hear you got hit by a car on Duval last night."

"It wasn't anything," Marlow waved a hand dismissively.

"Are you sure about that?" Jamie asked.

61

"Not really, but I do think it was just a coincidence."

"So, tell me about it."

"I got the feeling that I was being followed and went back to Mallory Square and hid. There was a guy that once he couldn't spot me headed back for Duval. I trailed him until I got knocked into the street, and then he was gone. I came home, had a drink and fell asleep during a movie," Marlow shrugged.

"So, you're no closer to finding the missing girl."

"Nope, but I have a feeling that somebody that knows something is starting to take notice," Marlow replied as he ran water into the coffee pot. He put grounds in a filter and put it in place then added the water to the coffee maker and turned it on. It wasn't long before the aroma of French vanilla filled the kitchen.

"Rick, do I need to tell you to be careful?" Jamie asked.

"Walter already has."

"How is the old man?" Gutierrez asked.

"He is doing well. Lola is after him to retire but he is refusing so far," Marlow shrugged. The pot was half full, so he pulled it out and filled two mugs before putting it back.

"You know that Walter is not going to be around forever?"

"I know that."

"So, what will you do once he's gone?"

"Same thing I'm doing now except I'll have to find another office."

"Just like that?"

"Pretty much. Walter's been like a second father to me, Jamie. But when he's gone, I'll mourn and then move on. That's what people do. I'm no different," Marlow shrugged.

"Are you still talking to Dr. Harmon?"

"Not for a while now."

"Maybe you should, pal," Gutierrez told him.

"I'll think about it."

"Do that. Something is off about you since Irma hit."

"My first real hurricane. I'll get over it."

"I hope so."

"Have you seen Elise lately?" Marlow asked, hoping to change the subject."

"A time or two on the street, but not to talk to. Keeping the island policed keeps me busy," Gutierrez shrugged.

"I'm sure it does. How about I meet you at 'Harpoon Harry's' in half an hour for breakfast?" Marlow asked.

"See you there, pal. Be careful," Jamie said, standing and walking to the door. Marlow locked it behind him and headed for the shower. Maybe he should give Jessica Harmon a call. She had helped him a lot after Della Martin had killed herself. Della had been the first woman he had loved after his shooting up in New York City. She had watched a friend and a woman that she was protecting get raped and murdered after being rendered helpless herself. It had been too much for her to live with and she had eaten her gun in true cop fashion. Something that he had never completely forgiven himself for. He felt that he should have spotted the signs.

Marlow shook the memory out of his head. This was not time to get bogged down in the baggage of his past. Not when he had a missing girl to find. He went to the bathroom, shaved, showered and got dressed. He fed Misty and made sure she had a full bowl of water before heading out the door.

Lost Girl

~ ~ ~

Jamie Gutierrez had driven straight to 'Harpoon Harry's' after leaving Marlow's place. He was worried about his friend. Marlow seemed to be acting more reckless than ever these past few days. He wondered if it was because Tina had been away, testifying at that trial. She was a good and calming influence on Marlow. He ordered a *café con leche* while he waited on Marlow to arrive.

He had also done a little looking into the missing girl, though he hadn't mentioned it to Marlow. He had verified that Quinn Kerns had arrived on Key West but could find no evidence that she had ever left. That meant that she had to still be on the island somewhere. But where? That was the question!

~ ~ ~

Ron greeted Marlow when he walked in and told him where Gutierrez was sitting in the back. Ron made it a point to greet most of his customers on a daily basis. Marlow nodded to Michael Haskins and Mick Murphy as he passed their table, and both men nodded back.

Jamie was halfway through his first *café con leche* when Marlow dropped into the chair across from him. "You're early," Jamie said looking at his watch.

"It happens," Marlow shrugged.

"So, where are you on the Quinn Kerns case?"

"I haven't found her yet."

"Any leads?"

"I talked to the girl she was staying with. She told me that Quinn had met some guy at the beach, but she didn't know who it was."

"And you still looking?"

"I am. I have some of my Baker Street Irregulars looking for her too," Marlow replied.

"Your what?" Gutierrez looked confused.

"They are a network of street kids and homeless kids around the island. Walter coined the name based on an old Sherlock Holmes story."

"That sounds like Walter. Have they turned up anything yet?"

"Not so far. I hope to hear from them later today."

"When will Tina be back?"

"She should have landed in Miami last night and will be driving home today."

"Glad to hear it, my friend. She centers you."

"She does. Without Tina, I feel like an unmoored boat drifting in a turbulent sea."

"I gathered. That was actually almost poetic, amigo."

"Thanks, I think," Marlow replied. The waitress arrived with two breakfast specials and a *café con leche* for each of them. It was a few minutes after eight a.m.

~ ~ ~

Tina Cord had gotten up early, showered and dressed, and had breakfast at the hotel. Her car had not been touched by the hurricane in the Miami International Airport's long-term parking. She climbed in and started the drive back to Key West. The normal three hour drive was probably going to take longer since the hurricane, but that was all right with her.

She was worried about Rick. Something about this case was eating away at him. She knew that he had missed her while she was gone, but it was more than that. With luck, she would be back on the island by noon.

~ ~ ~

Quinn screamed against her gag as the man entered her from behind. She felt her anus ripping as he forced himself inside her. It hurt! It hurt bad! Her hands clawed at the ropes that bound her wrists to the bed posts. It was bad enough when he and his brother raped her vaginally, but this was worse. He was showing her that he was the one with the power and there was nothing that she could do about it. She felt the blood mixing with his fluids inside her, felt his member swelling as he got ready to explode. Then it happened, and as he shrank, her muscles forced him out of her. Tears fell from her eyes as the pain overwhelmed her and her shame filled her heart.

~ ~ ~

Rocco had managed to find a few girls that had met Quinn. Marlow would be happy to hear that. One of them had seen her talking to an older guy who was maybe thirty. That was information that Marlow would want to have. He dialed Marlow's cell and passed him the news and the girl's name. It made him feel a little weird working for the private eye. But that was okay. Marlow had managed to keep him from getting in trouble with the cops. Rocco sighed. Marlow had kept him from getting arrested and he owed the guy. Marlow could have easily turned him in, but he had chosen not to. He had always wondered about that but had never gotten the nerve to ask Marlow directly.

Chapter Eight

After finishing their breakfasts, the two men separated with the chief heading for the police station and Marlow heading for the office. He was troubled by some of the questions that Jamie had brought up, and that troubled him. The fact that they troubled him as much as they did, made him realize that they were distracting him at a time when he could not afford to be distracted.

He had to find Quinn Kerns and he had to keep from being killed while doing so. He wished he had a cigarette but had given them up after Della Martin had killed herself. It was his own small way of honoring her memory. Except, the cravings never really went away. He fought them on a daily basis. Tina being gone only made them worse. He would be glad when she got home.

He walked to his car and climbed in and drove to Walter's house. The large two-story house had served Walter as a home and office for more than forty years. Walter's children had grown up in the house, and his wife had died there. Walter had remained there, and Lola had finally moved in with him. That brought a smile to his face. Lola was only a few years older than Marlow, but she had loved her boss for many years and he had finally realized his own feelings for her after his heart attack and the attempts on his life by his youngest daughter. That had been a messy bit of business. He shook his head at the memory as he climbed out of his car and headed for the outer office door that was his private entrance into the house.

His cell phone rang, and Marlow answered it. It was Rocco. "What have you got, Rocco?" he asked.

"I found a couple of girls that knew Quinn."

"That's good news."

"I got something else too."

"What is it?"

"One of them saw him talking to an older guy in his thirties, and she's pretty sure that she can describe him," Rocco told him. Marlow felt elated for the first time since he had taken the case.

"Come by Walter's office. Lola will have an envelope for you. Now, give me the names," Marlow told him.

Marlow had put the names in his computer as soon as he had it booted up. As each name was being looked up, he got out five twenties and put it in an envelope, sealed it, wrote Rocco's name on it and carried it up to the reception desk and handed it to Lola.

"What's this?" Lola asked eyeing the envelope.

"A reward for information. I told Rocco to come by and that you would have it for him."

"Let me guess, he's one of your 'Irregulars'?" Lola asked.

"He's their leader," Marlow grinned before walking back to his office. He knew that his informal network of young informants was an object of consternation for his boss's secretary. Both he and Walter found it amusing.

He had three more names to add to the list. Stacy James, Nina Thomas, and Vera Cook. They were all Quinn's age which was a plus. She would have gravitated to them, maybe even more than to Kieran, who she lived with. He picked up his phone and dialed the police department. He asked for the chief when the switchboard answered.

"What have you got, Marlow?" Chief Gutierrez asked.

"I have witnesses that knew Quinn Kerns, and one who saw her getting chatty with a guy in his mid to late thirties. She says that she can describe him," Marlow announced.

"That would be very helpful."

"I thought so." Marlow agreed.

"So, what are you going to do?"

"Talk to them. You want to go along?"

"No, but I'll send you a detective in case you need backup. She's a new hire from up in Miami. Angelica Sharp," Jamie told him.

"Have her meet me at Walter's office," Marlow told him. He poured himself another cup of coffee and he leaned back in his chair. Three names, all of them young girls. Jamie had the right idea sending him a female detective. She would make the girls feel more at ease and give him the protection of an adult female in case any of the girls tried to claim that he made a move on them. Not that he would. He had his standards and underage girls weren't on his lists of interest other than for the information on Quinn that they could provide him with.

~ ~ ~

Detective Angelica Sharp wasn't sure that was up when the chief called her into his office. He was going through some papers on his desk when she entered.

"Chief," she said to get his attention. He looked up at her, his brown eyes appraising.

"Have a seat," he told her, nodding to the chairs on the opposite side of his desk. Detective Sharp did so. She was wearing a sleeveless pink cotton blouse and jeans. She had on Nike running shoes. She took a seat and waited.

Finally, he stacked the papers and closed the folder and sat back to regard her. "I suppose you're wondering why I called you in here."

"It had crossed my mind, Sir," Angelica replied.

"I want you to go to the offices of Walter Loomis and meet with his investigator, Rick Marlow. He's hunting for a young teenage girl that went missing right before Irma hit. He's going to interview three underage girls and he wants a witness."

"Okay, but why me?" she asked.

"You're the only female detective I have, and I think you'll be able to get more out of the girls than he can. I've already opened a case file on the missing girl and you are taking lead on it. Marlow is ex-NYPD and he knows what he's doing," Chief Gutierrez told her.

"So, you want me to work with him?" She asked for clarification.

"Yes. We don't need girls going missing on our island. The Key West Chamber of Commerce doesn't like the negative publicity."

"Do you have an address for this Loomis guy?"

"Right here," the chief replied handing her a post-it note.

"Okay. Do you want a report when I get back?"

"Write it up and send it to my computer," he told her.

Angelica shop nodded and walked out of his office heading for the elevator. She had heard stories about this Marlow guy. Most of them good. It would be nice to finally put a face to the legend.

~ ~ ~

He was back at work, still helping with the cleanup. It didn't require thinking, and he was able to do it like a mindless automaton. His thoughts drifted, going back to Quinn and the pleasure he had taken with her the night before.

Marlow was going to be a problem and he was proving to be difficult to kill. He was going to have to get more creative. Marlow was going to mess up everything if he kept digging around. Maybe it was time to find a better way to eliminate the private eye.

~ ~ ~

Marlow was talking to Lola when Detective Sharp arrived at Walter's office. He wasn't prepared for her looks. She was a tall blond with blue eyes and she filled her shirt and jeans out nicely. "Are you Marlow?" she asked, giving him the once over.

"Rick Marlow, at your service," he replied.

"Chief Gutierrez sent me."

"You're the detective that is to assist me when talking to the three girls that were close to Quinn Kerns before she disappeared?"

"Yes."

"Then, let's go," he told her heading out the door, leaving her to follow him to a red Ford Focus sedan. It was an older model, a 2002, and it was starting to show some rusting from the salt air.

71

Once inside, Marlow started it up and rolled down the window and started the air-conditioner. As soon as it started blowing cold air, he rolled up his window and backed out of the driveway and headed for Smathers Beach because that was where Rocco had told him he would find the three girls. He looked over at her. "You got a name?" he asked.

"Angelica Sharp," she replied.

"Angel it is, then," Marlow said with a grin, knowing it would annoy her.

"I hate that."

"I don't give a rat's ass," Marlow told her.

"You really are an asshole," Angelica replied.

"Everybody says that sooner or later," Marlow told her.

~ ~ ~

It didn't take long to reach the beach, and Marlow parked on the road. Families and teens were scattered all over the sand. The sky was a bright blue overhead, and the sun beat down on the sand, reflecting off of it. Marlow led the way out onto the sand. Rocco had given him a very vivid description of the girls and the bathing suits that they wore. It didn't take long to find them.

Marlow knelt down in the sound and identified himself, as well as mentioning that Rocco had sent him. "Stacy, what can you tell me about Quinn Kerns?" he asked.

~ ~ ~

Silas Drago headed for Key West. He had been promised good money to get rid of a peeper down on 'the rock.' Things had been getting stale in Miami. So, the opportunity for a change of scenery had seemed like a good idea. He was going to pick up Pete Granger at Marathon on the way down. They had done muscle work together before and had become friends. Drago was built like a body builder with shoulder-length dark hair. His eyes were an icy blue. He had been a leg-breaker for a large number of crooks in his time.

~ ~ ~

Tina was tired when she pulled up in front of her apartment. She always hated driving from Miami to Key West. The ordeal in Chicago had been almost as painful as what she had gone through while she was being stalked. She shivered at the memory. She shut off the car, unbuckled her seatbelt and opened the door. The heat and humidity hit her like a wet towel to the face. She locked the car, unlocked the trunk to take out her luggage and dragged it to her front door. Unlocking it, she pulled the suitcase inside and shut the door behind her.

The air was comfortably cool inside, and she breathed it in deeply. She pulled out her cell phone and dialed Marlow's number. He answered on the first ring. "Please tell me you're at home," he said.

"I am. It sounds like you have missed me."

"Like a dog without a bone. I'll be there in twenty minutes. I can't wait to see your beautiful face."

"I'll be here," she told him, smiling as she hung up. She then dragged the suitcase to the laundry room and started putting her clothes in the wash. She had enjoyed being home with family in Chicago, but she discovered she had missed the island and Marlow even more. Chicago was no longer her home. Key West was. She was officially an island girl. Smiling, Tina shook her head while she separated colors and white and put them into wash.

~ ~ ~

Marlow arrived exactly twenty minutes from when he told her he would. He practically ran to the door and went inside. "Hey there," he said, grinning at her. She ran into his arms and jumped up, her arms going around his neck as her legs wrapped around his waist as she mashed her lips against his.

Moments later, they were on the bed, naked together, each acting as if they were starved for the other. The first time was fast and feverish, like someone dehydrated craving water. The second time was slower and personal, each of them taking their time as they drained every bit of pleasure that they could from each other.

Finally, they both lay back, side by side, exhausted. "Well, you *did* miss me," Tina whispered, still breathing hard.

"You think?" Marlow grinned at her, his blue eyes twinkling.

"So, tell me about this new case you are working," Tina prodded him.

"There was a young girl named Quinn Kerns who ran away from an abusive father and came to Key West. She arrived here safely but vanished at some point when Irma hit. There is no record of her leaving the island. I spoke to some of her friends today and they mentioned that she had met an older man, one in his early thirties. They haven't seen him around Smathers Beach lately, but they all had the sense that he was local," Marlow explained.

"What do you think?"

"I think she never left the island," Marlow told her.

"Why is that?" Tina asked.

"Because there is no record of it. I believe that she was kidnapped," Marlow said.

"Why?"

"Because it fits with my theory. I think that she was kidnapped and that she is still somewhere here on the island. If she is, I will find her, one way or another."

"What else has happened?"

"The first day on the job I was mugged. Then yesterday, I was dumped into the bay and when I got here, somebody tried to shoot me. I got a bullet into him, but he managed to get away."

"He was in my apartment?"

"Yes. But I made sure that it was secure after he left. I still haven't figured out exactly how he got in."

"Am I safe here?" Tina was suddenly concerned.

"As near as I can make you safe," Marlow replied.

Chapter Nine

"**W**hy don't I stay over at your place for few days?" Tina asked, still unnerved that someone had broken into her apartment while she was gone. It brought back memories of her stalker. He had also broken into her place. Marlow looked at her. Tina's face had gone pale her respiration had increased.

"That's fine with me, babe" Marlow told her, drawing her close in a hug. He kissed her forehead and just held her close, trying his best to make her feel safe. She had been through enough with Kurt Dawes. He had hounded her from Chicago to Key West, every place that she had thought she had been safe. She had just returned from Chicago and testifying against his twin brother who had stood in for him with his parole officer while his twin had hunted her like an animal to kidnap and try to kill her. Marlow had saved her along with Jessica Harmon, a psychiatrist that had helped them both. In fact, helping Tina had helped Jessica come back from her failure to predict that Della Martin would take her own life.

"Do you want me to call Jessica, and set up an appointment for you?" Marlow asked her as he held her close, feeling the beat of her heart pounding in time with his own.

"I think that might be a good idea," Tina murmured.

Just then Marlow's phone rang. He reached over and scooped it up, answering the call. "Marlow," he announced. He listened intently. "I'll be there in half an hour," he said breaking the connection. He looked at Tina. "You've got clothes at my place and Misty has been missing you. Get dressed you can take a shower there. I may have caught a break on the missing girl," he told her reaching for his pants.

"Find her, Ricky. Don't let anything more happen to her than what she has already been through," Tina told him, stepping into her panties and pulling them up. She reached for her bra.

"I'll do my best," Marlow told her, heading for the bathroom.

~ ~ ~

Exactly thirty minutes later he arrived at the Key West Police Department. He checked in at the front desk and was told to head on back to the elevator. He rode it up to the second floor where the Homicide Department was located. Detective Sharp was waiting on him.

"We may have a lead," she told him as he entered her cubicle.

"That's good news," Marlow agreed. "So, what is the lead?"

"Vera Cook was the only one that got a good look at the guy that Quinn had been hanging out with. Marie Goodwin sat down with her and did a sketch. This guy looks familiar, but I just can't quite place him. I'm hoping you might have better luck," Sharp explained.

"Okay," Marlow told her.

~ ~ ~

Georgie felt sorry for the girl. He knew that Oscar had hurt her last night, he had hurt her bad. It made Georgie feel bad. He liked Quinn. She seemed to understand him, even understand him better than Oscar ever had. He liked Quinn. She was nice to him. She told him it was okay to touch her as long as he was gentle. That made him happy.

~ ~ ~

Oscar looked at his phone checking to see if Drago had arrived from Miami yet. So far, there was no word. That bothered him. He was paying Drago good money to take care of his problem with Marlow, and it bothered the hell out of him that the man had yet to arrive on the island. He had done so much to build up his new identity at the end of the road. He had hoped that he would never be called to active duty again. So far, he had not, but this time it was thanks to his own mission. Some of his fellow cops were bound to figure it out, no matter what his disguise might be. They would turn on him, but it would be too late. Many of them would be dead.

~ ~ ~

Marlow watched as Marie worked. He realized that there was a very good chance that he would recognize the face once that she was done. Sure, it might be *a* second glimpse but there was a strong possibility that it would be enough. He took the paper from her hand and studied the face. It was familiar all right, but he was having a hard time believing it. "Do you recognize him?" Sharp asked him.

"Yes. It looks like Steve Lorca," Marlow told her.

"Who?" Sharp asked innocently, obvious she didn't

recognize the name. Maybe that was a good thing. Because it might give Marlow a chance to reach him first and get Lorca to tell him where Quinn Kerns was.

"A guy I met doing cleanup after the storm. I don't know where he lives, though."

"Hit the street, and you had damn well better call if you find him!" Sharp snapped at him.

"You'll be my first call," he promised, as he turned and headed back towards the elevator. He had no intention of keeping that promise. What he planned to do was find Lorca and beat the truth out of him!

~ ~ ~

Steve Lorca was using a chainsaw to cut up one of the many downed trees, this time down by the cemetery. He was working with a crew of five other guys and they were making good time on cutting up the tree. They might even finish the job by six o'clock in the evening.

That would be a good thing. It would give him time to clean up before his date with Connie Bishop. Connie was an actual 'Conch', and her family had been on the island for ages. Lorca had only arrived a few months ago. He had come to the island from Louisiana after getting out of the Marines. Steve had left 'the Big Easy' under a cloud after a fight in the French Quarter that had left a man dead and Lorca was covered in the dead man's blood. He had gotten out three steps ahead of an arrest warrant for murder.

He hadn't tried to kill Darjeen, but the man had given him no choice. Darjeen was trying to stab him and he had managed to turn the knife back on the guy. He shook his head. Darjeen was a local and Lorca known as a Yankee. They would have hung him if they had gotten the chance.

No, fleeing was the only choice that he had. So, he had come to 'the End of the Road' to see if maybe he couldn't start over and make a new life for himself.

~ ~ ~

Vera Cook was riding her bicycle home from the beach. She had pulled a tee shirt and shorts on over her bikini. Her curly dark hair was streaming out behind her when the man stepped out in front of her. She looked up but didn't have time to scream before his arm hit her in the chest and drove her backwards off of the bike. Her head it the pavement and everything went black.

~ ~ ~

Rocco was getting worried. He knew that Marlow had talked to the girls, but he hadn't heard from any of the trio in a while. He pulled out his cell phone and dialed Nina Thomas. She picked up on the first ring. "Hey, Rocco," Nina answered.

"Did you guys talk to Marlow?" he asked.

"Yes, we did. Vera had actually saw the guy that Quinn was hanging out with and gave the police a description. She went with the lady cop, so she could talk to a sketch artist," Nina told him.

"So, why did I have to call you to find this out?" Rocco asked, impatiently.

"We didn't think it was that big a deal," Nina shrugged.

"It is," Rocco barked at her before hanging up. He dialed Marlow's number and waited for the gumshoe to pick up.

~ ~ ~

"What have you got, Rocco?" Marlow asked when he answered.

"Is Vera with you?" Rocco asked.

"No, but she gave the sketch artist a good description of who to look for," Marlow replied.

"She's not answering her phone."

"Do you know where she lives?"

"Yeah, I do."

"Go there, make sure she's okay. If you see Steve Lorca, call me," Marlow told him before hanging up.

~ ~ ~

Oscar dragged the girl into hiding. It wouldn't do to have her body found too quickly. But with her dead, there was nobody that could actually identify him. He had seen the sketch, and while it was close, it looked more like a guy named Steve Lorca than it did of him. It would be easy enough to put the blame on Lorca and nobody would be the wiser. This was a good thing, because it would make sure that nobody was looking at him.

He had gotten her name at headquarters, had watched from a distance as she had described him to the sketch artist. It had been a small matter to follow her when she left the station to where she was alone and there was nobody around to see. Her struggles were growing weaker and he held the silk kerchief tightly around her neck, the knot in the cloth pressing her windpipe closed, effectively cutting off her air intake.

When she was dead, he stuffed her behind some bushes near the cemetery and peeled off his gloves and returned to his patrol car. It was time to start work for the night.

~ ~ ~

Marlow was on his bicycle peddling like crazy for Vera's house, knowing that Rocco would probably beat him there.

He hoped that the girl was there safe and sound, because if she was harmed, it would be on him!

Marlow cut past the cemetery and spotted a police car turning off onto a side street three or four blocks away. From the speed he was traveling and the bumps in the road he couldn't be sure. Tree crews had been working near the graveyard today. He wondered if Steve Lorca had been one of them. He pushed the thought from his head as he skidded the bicycle around a corner and shot down a cross street. Rocco was standing on Vera's front porch, talking to her mother when Marlow reached the driveway and braked his bike to a stop. He climbed off and put down his kickstand and walked up to the porch. Vera's mother looked at him, it was clear from her expression that she was wondering who he was.

"Hello, Ma'am. My name is Marlow and I'm a private investigator. Rocco, your daughter, and some other kids are trying to help me find a missing girl," he said by way of introduction.

"Do you know where Vera is?" she asked, her face showing her concern.

"I came straight here when Rocco called and told me that he hadn't been able to get in touch with her," Marlow explained.

"Then, you don't know where she is either?" Mrs. Cook asked.

"I don't. I know the police spoke to her and she described a man to the sketch artist that rendered a pretty good picture of a suspect," Marlow told her.

"We need to call the police," Mrs. Cook said, shaking her head.

"I think that would be a good idea. Why don't you go inside and do that?" Marlow suggested. She nodded and disappeared inside the house. Marlow grabbed Rocco's arm and guided them a few steps away from the door. "Were you able to reach the others?"

"They made it home okay," Rocco replied.

"That's something anyway," Marlow nodded.

"Yeah, but I'm scared that maybe it isn't enough," Rocco admitted, a tear running down his cheek.

"Me, too, kid. Me too," Marlow sighed. It didn't take long before several police cars pulled up out front, including two units from the sheriff's department. Detective Sharp was one of the first people to approach the house where Marlow and Rocco kept vigil over the shaken Mrs. Cook.

~ ~ ~

"What's going on, Marlow?" Sharp asked him, as she walked up.

"The witness that was able to give the description of the guy Quinn Kerns was seeing, it seems that she never made it home," Marlow explained.

"That can't be good," Sharp shook her head.

"I don't think so either. I think that we should get search teams out all across the island."

"You think she's dead?"

"I think that there is a good chance of it."

"That sucks."

"Yes, it does," Marlow agreed.

~ ~ ~

Tina Cord made herself at home in Marlow's apartment. It wasn't as nice as hers, but that was okay. Misty, the cat, curled around her legs and she bent down and picked the up the gray fur ball and it started to purr loudly.

"I've missed you, too," Tina whispered to the cat as she hugged into her chest. Tina settled on the couch and turned on the television, flipping through the channels as she tried to find something to watch.

Finally, she settled on a rerun of *Tammy and the Bachelor*. Marlow had gotten her hooked on old movies. Misty curled up in her lap and was soon fast asleep.

Chapter Ten

It didn't take long to gather a number of island residents to join in the hunt for the missing Vera Cook. Sharp had taken her back to Smathers Beach after she had worked with the sketch artist. Marlow and Rocco had taken a group to the beach and were working their way back to Vera's house. Sharp was at the house with Vera's mother asking questions about the teen and her habits. Other cops were leading groups in searching the neighborhood where Vera lived.

"Marlow, do you think something happened to Vera?" Rocco asked him.

"As much as I hate to say it . . . yes, I do," Marlow replied.

"If something has happened to her, you'll find out who did it, right?"

"You can take that to the bank, Rocco," Marlow replied, meaning it.

"Thank you for that. I didn't think she could get hurt when I asked her for help."

"It's not your fault, Rocco. If anybody is to blame it's me for having you ask around about Quinn," Marlow sighed. The sun was starting to sink into the horizon.

"Hey, that's her bike!" Rocco pointed to a ten speed lying on the sidewalk.

"Are you sure?" Marlow asked.

"Positive."

"Let's go check it out," Marlow said, a bad feeling filling his gut. He had a pretty good idea about what they were going to find. It would be especially hard on Rocco. A tall hedge grew alongside the road. They were very near the cemetery.

They were almost to the hedge when the smell hit him. Marlow touched Rocco's shoulder. "Stay here," he warned him. There was a break in the hedge. Marlow stepped through it. It didn't take long to find the young woman's body. Her bladder and bowels had evacuated when she died, and the heat had started the decomposition working quicker.

Marlow pulled out his cell phone and called Sharp, telling in short concise sentences what he had found. She promised to be there in a few minutes. Marlow snapped pictures of the body with his cell phone, as well as the ground surrounding it. Then, he went back through the hedge to tell Rocco the bad news.

"Marlow?" Rocco looked at him, his eyes wide.

"She's dead, kid. Sharp and the Crime Scene Unit are on their way, as well as the sheriff's department homicide unit," Marlow told him. Rocco dropped to his knees, letting out and anguished cry, tears flowing from his eyes and running down his cheeks.

It hurt Marlow to see the kid like that. Especially, since he knew that he was the root cause. He never should have asked Rocco to ask around about Quinn. Now, Vera Cook was dead, and he wasn't really any closer to finding Quinn. Sure, he had somebody to talk to, but that wasn't iron clad. Still, he wanted to find Steve Lorca in the worst possible way and ask him some questions about Quinn Kerns.

~ ~ ~

Detective Sharp started barking out orders to her people as soon as she arrived, and it didn't take long for the crime scene tape to go up. Marlow had sent Rocco and the rest of the searchers home after calling the police. A few had hung around anyway, curiosity getting the better of them. Marlow was tired, and he needed a drink. This case was getting more complicated by the day. He pulled out his cell and dialed Tina. She answered on the first ring.

"What's going on, Rick?" she asked.

"One of my teen informants is dead after describing a guy that Quinn Kerns was hanging out with," Marlow told her.

"How are you doing?" Tina asked.

"I'm feeling guilty as hell for getting the street kids involved."

"Would you have a possible suspect without them?" Tina asked.

"No," Marlow sighed.

"It is not your fault, Ricky."

"Why am I having a hard time believing that?"

"Because you are too close to it. You need to take a step back and look at it objectively," Tina told him.

"That is kind of hard for me to do right now."

"I know that."

"Come home. Let it go for tonight and look at it fresh in the morning."

"That sounds remarkably like a good idea," Marlow told her before hanging up. He walked over to Sharp. "Are you done with me?" he asked.

"For now. You've given your statement, right?" Sharp asked him.

"I have. If you need me for anything else, call me at the office in the morning," Marlow told her.

"Will do," Sharp agreed and Marlow went back to the Cook's, grabbed his bicycle and peddled home.

"How was your day?" Tina asked as he entered his duplex.

"Let me grab a beer first," Marlow told her. He noticed that an old movie 'Treasure of the Sierra Madres' was playing on television as he headed for the kitchen.

"Bring me one too, please," Tina called after him. Marlow pulled two bottles of Killian's Red out of the fridge, twisted the tops off and dropped the bottle caps in the trash. He then carried both bottles back into the living room handed her one and then rounded the couch to take a seat beside her.

"One of the young women that had seen the man that Quinn Kerns had made friends with was murdered after giving the guy's description to a sketch artist," Marlow said. Tina's hand flew to her mouth.

"Oh, my God," she gasped.

"I can't help but feel that on some level it is my fault. It nearly crushed Rocco. I think that he liked Vera Cook a lot."

"Don't blame yourself, Ricky. You had no way of knowing something like this would happen."

"No, but I should have. I had no idea that there would

be this kind of collateral damage."

"Here," Tina said, pulling his head down to rest on her breast and she held him and did her best to provide comfort.

~ ~ ~

Steve Lorca had cleaned up and had picked up Connie Bishop and they had driven north to the town of Marathon on Vaca Key. "You are in for a treat tonight," Steve told her.

"Really? And what is that?" Connie smiled at him.

"Eric Stone is playing at the Rusty Anchor Bar and Grill. He is a phenomenal singer," Steve told her.

"I've heard the name of the singer, but not the venue," Connie said, her nose wrinkling in thought.

"Rusty is and old friend. Him and his pal, Jesse McDermitt, were in my unit once upon a time," Steve told her.

"You were a soldier?"

"I was more than that. I was a U.S. Marine, Force Recon," Steve said proudly. "I wasn't always a beach bum."

"Who was?" Connie asked lightly, her eyes smiling. The parking lot of the Rusty Anchor was filled to overflowing and they had to walk a ways to get inside. The patio was at capacity and the overflow had moved into the bar proper. Steve found them a table, deposited Connie and headed for the bar to grab him a beer.

"Hey, Rusty!" Steve called when he reached the bar. Rusty raised his grizzled red head and instantly recognized his old comrade in arms.

"Steve! How the hell have you been?" Rusty demanded.

"I've been good. Working on shrimp boats down on Key Weird," Steve told him.

91

"Too bad Jesse isn't around, he'd love to see you," Rusty told him.

"Can I get a couple of beers? I brought a date up to listen to Eric play."

"Not a problem, buddy. Why do you want?"

"Give me a couple of Red Stripes," Steve told him.

"Coming right up," Rusty told him.

Seconds later Steve arrived back at the table where he had left Connie with two ice cold bottles of Red Stripe beer. He sat one on the table in front of her. Music began to flow out of the speakers as Eric Stone began his first set.

~ ~ ~

Georgie looked at the girl. Her name was Quinn, and he had grown fond of her. He didn't like what Oscar had done to her last night. He could tell that Oscar had hurt her. It made him angry. Quinn didn't deserve being hurt like that.

He would not let Oscar hurt her like that again. Quinn had been nice to him, she didn't complain when he was with her. She had complimented him on how gentle he was with her. It made him feel good. Quinn talked to him like she was his real girlfriend, not just a pretend one.

~ ~ ~

A storm rolled in during the night. Marlow lay awake long after Tina had gone to sleep. He still couldn't rid himself of the vision of Vera Cook dead on the ground with a silk scarf knotted tightly around her neck. She was dead because of him. Because he had asked questions trying to find Quinn Kerns.

Vera was dead, but Quinn was out there, somewhere in the night, suffering through God only knew what. He prayed that he would find her alive, but he hoped that her pain was at an end.

Marlow slipped out from under the covers without disturbing Tina and made his way to the kitchen. He took a six ounce tumbler from the freezer where he kept it cold and poured three fingers of vodka into it. He took it to the couch and sipped at it. Soon, the glass was empty, and he was sound asleep.

~ ~ ~

Marlow opened his eyes to bright sunlight streaming in through the windows and pain lancing through his skull like somebody was pounding it with a railroad spike. He could hear Tina in the kitchen and it sounded like she was slamming doors and pans around. Misty jumped up on his chest, looked down at him with wide green eyes and let out a roar worthy of the iconic MGM lion.

Marlow put her down on the floor and rolled to a sitting position, tossing aside the light blanket that Tina had apparently covered him with. His tongue felt like he had been giving Misty a bath with it. He got up and staggered to the bathroom, dropping his shorts and sitting on the toilet as he did his business. He flushed, turned on the shower and grabbed a bottle of Aspirin from the medicine chest. He dry swallowed them before striping off his shorts and getting into the shower.

Twenty minutes later, he walked into the kitchen where Tina was putting breakfast on the table. "You deserted me last night," she said.

"I was having trouble sleeping and I didn't want to wake you. You've been through enough lately," Marlow told her.

"I thought we were a team, Ricky. We share our

problems and work them out together otherwise it doesn't work for us."

"I know. I just couldn't get Vera Cook out of my head. Realistically, I know I had nothing to do with her death. But in my heart, I feel responsible."

"I know you do, but you have to be realistic. Vera died because she saw the man who took Quinn and then she talked to the police. You could not have foreseen that."

"Maybe," Marlow took a sip of his coffee. "Are you going back to work today?" he asked, changing the subject.

"Yes, I am. I think it will be better for me than sitting around here all day."

"Let's eat and then I will drop you off at Pepe's before I head to the office."

Tina kissed him. "That sounds like a plan."

~ ~ ~

Steve Lorca was driving home from Connie's place when he noticed a patrol car sitting out in front of his house. What was that about? He had a bad feeling about it.

He turned off the street before the cop could see him. Where the hell was he going to go? It was starting to feel like New Orleans all over again. What was the name of that lawyer Marlow worked for? Walter something. Loomis! That was it, Walter Loomis! Lorca pulled out his cell phone and looked up the address for Loomis's office. He headed there.

Chapter Eleven

Lola Ponsberry flagged Marlow down as soon as he came through the front door. "What's going on?" he asked.

"We just got a new client, and I'm not sure you're going to be happy about it," the vivacious redhead told him.

"Why would I be upset?"

"His name is Steve Lorca."

"Wow. I've been looking for him," Marlow nodded, frowning.

"Apparently, so have the police. He spotted two cars sitting on his house and came straight here and hired Walter."

"What is your impression of him?"

"I think that he really may be innocent."

"Is he in with Walter now?"

"He is."

"Okay. I'm going in," Marlow told her ,as he started towards the conference room. Marlow knocked twice before opening the door and stepping inside.

~ ~ ~

"Ricky how good of you to join us. I believe you know Mr. Lorca?" Walter Loomis asked.

"We've met," Marlow nodded.

"Excellent. It appears that Mr. Lorca is a person of interest in the disappearance of Quinn Kerns," Walter explained.

"Imagine that, since a witness described him as talking to the missing woman and then she turned up murdered last night." Marlow said softly.

"I had nothing to do with that," Lorca told him.

"Nobody said you did," Walter told him, giving Marlow his version of the evil eye.

"Do you know Quinn Kerns?" Marlow asked.

"I know who she was, but I never talked to her."

"What about the police sketch? It looks like you," Marlow pointed out.

"Sure, it looks like me and dozens of other guys on 'the rock'," Lorca countered.

"Okay, and if I accept that, what can you tell me about the girl?"

"She hung around looking for somebody that could take care of her. It was obvious that she had little in the way of street smarts. She was on the run and scared. I recommended a couple of shelters to her and then she was gone. That is the sum total of my involvement with Quinn Kerns," Lorca told him.

"Say I believe you? Where should I look next?" Marlow asked.

"There was a cop hanging around. I don't know his name and he resembles me," Lorca replied.

"That is awful thin," Marlow pointed out.

"You think I don't know that? That is why I hired Mr. Loomis!"

"Okay, Steve. I believe you. I'm going to talk to the

sheriff and see if I can't get you released into my custody," Marlow told him.

"You can do that?" Lorca asked.

"Walter can," Marlow told him. "First you need to turn yourself in for questioning."

"I'll make the call," Walter said, standing and heading for the reception desk.

"Marlow, listen. I promise you I had nothing to do with that girl's disappearance," Lorca said.

"The girl that talked to the sketch artist, she was murdered last night. Can you provide and alibi for where you were?" Marlow asked his face stone cold.

"As soon as I got off work, I went home and showered and then picked up Connie Bishop and we drove up to Marathon to the Rusty Anchor bar and grill to listen to Eric Stone. Rusty, the owner is an old Marine buddy and he'll vouch for me," Lorca said.

"That sounds easy enough to check out. Connie works with Tina at Pepe's. And a call to Marathon is no big deal."

"I didn't do this, Marlow," Lorca told him.

"I'll check your story. I suspect the cops will do the same. It sounds like you might be telling the truth, and somebody might be trying to frame you," Marlow sighed.

"I need you to find out."

"I'll do what I can."

"Chief Gutierrez and Detective Sharp are on their way to collect you. Ricky will drive me to the station, so I can be there when they question you, Mr. Lorca. After that, we'll see where we stand," Walter told him.

"That sounds very reasonable, Mr. Loomis."

"Call me Walter, dear boy."

"Sure thing, Walter," Lorca smiled for the first time since he had entered the lawyer's office. A short time later, Jamie and Detective Sharp arrived. Walter announced that he was representing Steve and after the man had been read his rights and handcuffed, Walter grabbed his briefcase and he and Marlow followed Lorca and the police outside. Lorca was loaded into an unmarked KWPD police car and Marlow and Walter climbed into the attorney's car and followed them to the police station.

"What are your impressions, Ricky?" Walter asked.

"As much as I first bucked at the idea, I believe him, Walter. I don't think he killed Vera Cook or took Quinn Kerns," Marlow sighed.

"Then you believe his story?"

"I haven't checked it out yet, but yeah, I do," Marlow told him.

"Then, step outside and see what you can do to verify his alibi," Walter told him.

"On it," Marlow replied. He turned and walked outside, leaving Walter waiting in the lobby.

~ ~ ~

"What are you thinking, Chief?" Sharp asked while Lorca was going through the booking process.

"I'm not sure what to think, Detective. I am very concerned about the missing girl. Missing girls and dead bodies are bad for tourism," Chief Gutierrez told her.

"I get that, Chief. I just don't like what is going on in my town."

"You aren't the only one," Jamie told her.

~ ~ ~

Quinn blinked back tears. She felt awful from the things

that had been done to her. Somebody had to be looking for her. Her parents . . . somebody. Hopefully, they would find her in time before the maniac and his halfwit brother ended up killing her!

Of the two, she preferred the halfwit brother. He was, at least, gentle with her and took his time to make sure that she was ready. His brother didn't care. She hoped and prayed that somebody would find her soon.

~ ~ ~

Tina was glad to be working again. To be honest, she had missed the business of her job at Pepe's. She liked waiting tables and she liked interacting with her customers. She had missed that while she had been away in Chicago.

Her cell chimed to let her know she had a text. She checked, and it was from Marlow asking about Connie Bishop. He wanted to know if she had been out with Steve Lorca the night before. Tina texted back that she would ask when Connie got to work, and promptly forgot about it.

~ ~ ~

Walter had managed to get Steve released on his own recognizance, and Steve had ridden with Walter and Marlow back to Walter's office. "Keep an eye out for anything unusual," Marlow had told the construction worker before he took his leave.

"I will. I promise," Steve said before he left. Walter looked at Marlow.

"What do you think?" he asked.

"I think he is innocent," Marlow sighed.

"Then, we both do. The question is what are we going to do about it?"

"That is the question, isn't it?"

"I'm afraid I have no answer," Walter said.

"Nor do I," Marlow admitted.

"Then, what are we going to do?"

"We find the bastard and we bring him down, one way or another," Marlow replied. He pulled out his phone and dialed Jessica Harmon.

~ ~ ~

"Marlow, it's been a while. How's Tina?" Jessica Harmon asked after she had answered the telephone.

"I'm calling about Tina. She just got back from testifying at the Kurt Dawes trial, and it has left her pretty shaken up. She's staying at my place right now. Is there any chance you might stop over and see her? I'll pay your rates," Marlow told her.

"I have no doubt. Let's just call this a free consultation for now. If it persists, then we'll get her back in for regular appointments," Jessica told him.

"I hope it doesn't come to that. Kurt Dawes nearly destroyed her."

"I know, Marlow. Even better than you. I'll go see her."

"Thank you, Jess," Marlow told her and broke the connection. Jessica sat back in her chair as she hung up her telephone. It had taken six months to get Tina to where she had a handle on her post-traumatic stress disorder. She hoped all of that work had not been undone by going back to Chicago where it had all started. Jessica grabbed her purse and keys and headed for the door.

~ ~ ~

Oscar had thought he was off the hook when he saw that Steve Lorca had been picked up. He had been in the station at the end of his shift and had hung around to see what would happen. He had been surprised to see Marlow and Walter Loomis walk into the station and go straight to the interrogation room where Lorca had been put. He was even more surprised to see Lorca walk out with Marlow and Loomis. After that, he had gotten the hell out of the station and went home.

Georgie and Quinn were both still asleep and he was too tired to have any fun with Quinn. What he needed was a good solid, eight hours of sleep.

~ ~ ~

Detective Evelyn Sharp looked over the reports one more time. She had been studying the murder book on Vera Cook for the past two hours. She had looked at Steve Lorca's alibi and it checked out which meant that he could not have been Vera Cook's killer. She hadn't yet dismissed him in the Quinn Kerns case, but she had a feeling that he wasn't involved.

She wasn't sure why she agreed with Marlow other than it fit the facts of the case. Vera Cook had been targeted. The question was why? She obviously had seen something more than what she had told the sketch artist, but what? It was an interesting question. Evelyn Sharp leaned back in her chair. She looked at the sketch again. It looked like Lorca sure, but it also looked like a few guys on the force. Could the killer actually be a cop? Who better to conceal evidence? She had a bad feeling as she got up and headed for the chief's office. If the killer was a cop, it would certainly explain a lot.

~ ~ ~

Tina Cord was working when she spotted Jessica Harmon enter Pepe's. She was pleased that Jessica took a seat in her section and she hurried over to give the doctor a menu. "Jess, what brings you here?" Tina asked.

"A little bird said you just got back from Chicago and testifying. I came by to see if you were okay," Jess told her.

"I don't know if I am or not," Tina said honestly.

"Why is that?" Jessica asked, as she followed Tina back up the stairs to Marlow's apartment.

"I'm having nightmares. Rick has been good about not mentioning it, but I know that he knows," Tina sighed.

"Why do you think that you are having these nightmares?"

"I wish I knew."

"Do you think they relate to Kurt Dawes?"

"They are all about him," Tina admitted.

"Kurt Dawes is dead, Tina. Marlow shot him outside your hotel room. You saw his dead body."

"I did, but in my mind, that doesn't mean that he is really dead," Tina admitted.

"Trust me, Tina, I saw his body. Kurt Dawes is really and truly dead," Jessica said.

"Do you believe in ghosts?" Tina asked.

"I'm not sure, Jessica admitted.

"Well, I am," Tina told her.

"Tina, be reasonable," Jessica said.

"I am. I looked into the devil's eyes and he was as real as you or me," Tina replied.

Chapter Twelve

Marlow frowned at his phone as it started to ring. He pulled it out of his pocket. It was a police department number. "Hello?"

"Marlow, Detective Sharp here. Where are you at right now?" she asked.

"I'm out in front of Key West Island Bookstore," Marlow replied.

"I need to talk to you, sooner would be better than later," Sharp replied.

"How about we meet at 'Harpoon Harry's'? It's about lunch time anyway."

"See you there in ten," Sharp told him. She hung up. Marlow wondered what was up. Sharp had sounded pretty serious. Marlow wondered if it had anything to do with the case as he headed for 'Harpoon Harry's'.

~ ~ ~

Sharp was waiting by the door when Marlow got there and watched as he chained his bike to the rack out front. "Lunch first," he told her, pushing open the door and waiting for her to enter.

They took a seat near the back and a waitress showed up with menus. Sharp ordered the lobster salad and Marlow had the patty melt with fries. Both ordered a *café con leche* for their drinks. The waitress vanished to give their order to the cook. Marlow look across the table at Sharp. "So, what's the deal?"

"What if the guy that Vera saw was a cop?" Sharp asked.

"That's a heck of a leap, from Lorca to a cop. Where did you come up with that idea?" Marlow asked.

"Was looking at the sketch, and I realized that there are at least three cops on the force that could be the guy in the sketch, and they are a lot closer than Steve Lorca."

"Do you know their names?"

"I can find out."

"You want me to take a look at them, don't you?" Marlow asked.

"I'd rather have you do it in case one of them is involved, rather than have internal affairs tip them off and maybe kill Quinn Kerns," Sharp replied.

"Good idea," Marlow admitted.

"I thought so."

"So, how soon can you get me the names?" Marlow asked her.

"I'll call you with them by the end of shift at five," Sharp told him. The waitress returned with their food. Once the server departed the table, they resumed their conversation.

"That sounds like a plan. I'll check them out and see if they have anything shady in their backgrounds. I'll let you know what I find. In the meantime, I'll keep looking for anyone that might have seen Vera before she was murdered," Marlow said.

"That seems like a good idea," Sharp nodded. They both attacked their food with gusto. Marlow picked up the check and he headed back to his apartment. He wanted to check on Tina. He was worried about her.

~ ~ ~

Jessica Harmon was waiting on the porch when Marlow got home. He chained his bike to the porch and took a seat beside her. Jessica looked grim. "How bad is it?" he asked.

"It's bad, Rick. Tina is convinced that Kurt Dawes is still alive and that he is still after her. She called him the devil," Jessica sighed.

"Okay, yeah, that is bad," Marlow admitted.

"Rick, Tina is in a bad place, a very bad place. This trial, it has messed with her head in a major way. I don't know if it was because Dawes was a twin or not. But she is scared shitless!"

"Yeah, I get that. What can I do to help her?"

"Be there for her, make her feel safe. If not, then I don't know what she might do."

"You mean she might end up like Della?" Marlow asked.

"It's possible, yeah." Harmon admitted.

"I'm not sure that I could go through that again," Marlow admitted.

"Me either," Jessica told him.

"So, what should I do?" he asked.

"Go up and talk to her. Be there for her," Harmon said.

~ ~ ~

Detective Sharp was back at the station. There were three officers that looked like the sketch and they were all on different shifts. She decided to look at the overtime rolls. They might give her a better view of what was going on.

Luke Kramer, Harry Noonan, and Peter Gregory. Those were the three guys that matched the sketch. She had spent some time gathering their names. Luke worked days, Harry afternoons, and Pete worked the graveyard shift.

Sharp considered checking their personnel files. Except that might set off alarms in the system. She knew that the chief was close with Marlow, and she hoped that it might give her some level of protection. No, it would be better to let Marlow look in on the background of the suspected cops.

~ ~ ~

Marlow headed up the stairs and entered his apartment. Tina was curled up on the couch, watching a soap opera. "How are you doing, kid?" Marlow asked.

"Not so good, Ricky. Did you send Jessica to see me?" Tina asked.

"I did. I was worried about you."

"Thank you," Tina pulled his head down and kissed him deeply. Marlow kissed her back, his hands settling on her hips and pulling her to him. Finally, they broke the kiss, both of them gasping for breath. "How did you know?" Tina asked him.

"You haven't been yourself since you got back. I didn't say anything, but I can tell. I was hoping you would say something, but you didn't. So, I called Jessica and asked her to check on you," Marlow explained.

"I tried, but you've been so busy with this case and trying to find that poor girl, I felt like she needed you more than I did," Tina shrugged.

"Tina, you are the most important person in my life. Please, don't ever forget that."

"Most of the time, I do. But ever since the trial, I've seen Kurt Dawes twice, and not just in my nightmares! I thought I saw him once in Miami, and then again here on the island since I got back. I was looking out the window at work and he was standing in the courtyard beside the building watching me. I blinked, and then he was gone," Tina started to cry.

"Honey, listen to me. Kurt Dawes is dead. You saw the body after I shot him in the head. There is no way he could have survived that," Marlow told her.

"Realistically, I know that, Ricky, but I also know that I have seen him twice. I know it's not his twin, because they took him straight to prison. I think he's haunting me. Kurt Dawes is the devil!"

"There has to be a reasonable explanation, Tina. And I will find it. You just have to give me a chance to do so."

~ ~ ~

He had the girl's address and her locks were easy enough to beat. He had hoped that she would be home and was disappointed when she was not. Then, he could have ended it and just slipped away. But she was making it a challenge now. Because of her, one of his brothers was dead and the other in prison. He couldn't let that go. She needed to pay for what she had done to his family!

~ ~ ~

Rocco was on his bike near the apartments where Marlow's girlfriend lived when he noticed some guy walking out of her apartment. The guy was big and muscular and had his head shaved and was a total stranger. Rocco had never seen him before. Marlow would probably want to know. Maybe he should follow the guy and see where he went. That way at least, he might be able to tell Marlow who the guy was. Rocco decided to follow him.

~ ~ ~

Evelyn Sharp had her three names. It hadn't been easy to get them without tipping anyone off. She was nervous. She hadn't even approached the chief with her suspicions. Only Marlow. She just wasn't sure who in the department that she could trust. She typed the names into a text message and sent it to Marlow. Hopefully, he would be able to narrow down their suspect list from the three names.

~ ~ ~

"Walter, are you feeling okay?" Lola Ponsberry asked her boss and lover. Sweat was beaded on his forehead and his face was pale.

"I'm not sure," Walter admitted.

"I should call your doctor."

"I . . . I think that might be a good idea," Walter said, sounding like he was having trouble breathing. Lola scooped up the phone and dialed 9-1-1. Ten minutes later, an ambulance was transporting Walter Loomis to the Lower Keys Medical Center. Lola rode in the ambulance with him.

~ ~ ~

Marlow answered his phone on the first ring. "Ricky, Walter has had another heart attack. We're at the Lower Keys Medical Center and they are talking about life flighting him to Miami," Lola told him.

"I'll be there as quick as I can get there," Marlow told her before hanging up.

"I'll come with you," Tina said, grabbing a jacket and heading for the stairs. Marlow was right behind her. They climbed into his Ford Focus and pulled out into the street.

Marlow parked, and he and Tina rushed inside heading for the ER. Lola stood forlornly in the waiting room. Marlow scooped her up in a big hug. "What's the word?" he asked.

"Nothing yet. I noticed that he was pale and sweating and suggested calling his doctor. He agreed, and I called 9-1-1. The EMT's said that it looked like a heart attack and brought him here. The doctor is with him now," Lola told them

"Walter is stronger than you think, he will be okay," Tina said, trying to comfort Lola. She was well aware of the bond between Lola and Walter.

"I hope so," Lola sighed.

"Walter's a tough old bird, Lola. Tougher than either of us realize. He will make it through this," Marlow said.

Just then, Thom Hark walked in. Thom was an old friend of Walter's. One of his oldest friends. Marlow had called him and told him of the lawyer's plight.

"How is the old boy?" Thom asked.

"Not good," Marlow told him.

"So, what is going on?" Thom asked.

"It appears that Walter has suffered from another heart attack," Lola said softly.

"Lola, I am so sorry," Thom told her.

"I've been trying to get him to slow down, but he is a very stubborn man."

"We are all very aware of that, Lola," Marlow told her.

~ ~ ~

Oscar woke up and it was dark outside. He headed for the shower and took a quick one. Quinn would have to wait until morning. It was time for him to go to work. He dressed in his uniform, packed his food and headed out the door. He had left written instructions for Georgie as to how to take care of Quinn while he was at work. It was getting close to time to get rid of Quinn and find another girl.

Quinn had been exceptional. He still enjoyed her, and the things that he had forced her to do for him. Georgie had not liked some of it, but that really didn't matter. Georgie was inconsequential. He was as useless as a tit on a boar. But he served his purpose.

~ ~ ~

Marlow paced back and forth in the waiting room. Tina sat, drinking a cup of coffee from one of the machines. It wasn't the worst that she had ever tasted, but it wasn't the best by a long shot. She had tried to get Ricky to settle down beside her, but she was having no luck with that. He was too concerned about Walter. Walter had given him a chance, when nobody else had. It was Walter who had gotten Marlow to clean up his act, when nobody else could.

Chapter Thirteen

Marlow looked up as the doctor came out to talk to them. "How is he?" Marlow asked with a slight tremor in his voice.

"He's had another heart attack but he's resting comfortably. Your fast action in calling 9-1-1 is why he is still alive. He's stable, but not out of the woods yet. Which one of you is Lola?" he looked around and Lola stood up.

"I am," she said softly.

"He's been asking for you. If you want to go on back, a nurse will take you to his room."

"Thank you, Doctor," Lola said moving past him. Marlow waited until Lola was past the swinging double doors before pinning the doctor with his gaze.

"Okay, Doc, how bad is it? Really?" Marlow asked.

"His heart stopped twice before we got him stabilized. Mr. Loomis is going to have to change his lifestyle, starting with his diet immediately or he will not live out the year. I assume you are Rick Marlow?"

"I am." Rick answered.

"Mr. Loomis told me that you are to contact Hiram Shapiro, his personal attorney. He said to speak with Mr. Shapiro and he would take things from there," the doctor said.

"It sounds to me like things might be worse than what you're telling us," Marlow said.

"It's pretty much in God's hands now, Mr. Marlow. I've done everything I can. Oh, and if Mr. Loomis makes it through the night, we are transferring him up to Miami General."

"Thanks, Doc," Marlow said soberly, turning and walking back over to where Tina and Thom waited.

"Well?" Thom asked, breaking the silence.

"It is bad. If he makes it through the night, they are transferring him up to Miami General. He told me to get a hold of Hiram Shapiro. Do you know him, Thom?"

"Yes, he and Walter are close friends. I'll be happy to introduce you."

"I appreciate that, Thom."

"How are *you* doing, Ricky? I know that you love Walter like a father," Tina said. Marlow nodded, as he dropped into the chair beside her.

"Honestly, Tina, I don't know." Marlow bent over and put his face in his hands.

~ ~ ~

Walter Loomis looked whiter than the sheets on the hospital bed he was lying in. His watery blue eyes were open when Lola entered the room, an oxygen tube in his nose. He smiled weakly at her as she took a seat next to the bed and reached over to take his plump hand in hers. "I'm sorry, my dear," Walter said, his voice barely above a whisper.

"You don't need to apologize, honey, you just need to get better," Lola told him.

"I'm not sure I can, dear Lola. I've lived a good life, one

that has been even better thanks to you."

"I don't want to lose you, Walter. I love you too much."

"Then, once I am back on my feet, will you marry me?" he asked her.

"Of course, I will," Lola leaned over and kissed him on the lips.

"Then, I will also be announcing my retirement before the wedding," Walter smiled at her.

"I think that will help," Lola nodded, tears running from her eyes.

~ ~ ~

Oscar showered and ate a good breakfast. Georgie was pretty quiet for a change. However, Oscar didn't say anything. It was something of a relief for his halfwit brother was usually babbling about everything and anything. Oscar had checked on Quinn and she was still safely locked up.

He would kill her and dump her over the weekend. He was already looking for another girl to take her place. One of the best things about being a cop was that nobody would suspect him of being responsible for things like this.

~ ~ ~

Rocco followed the man that he had seen leaving Tina Cord's apartment to Duval Street. It was late, but the street was still packed with the partiers and the tourists who came for the party atmosphere. The guy was over six feet tall, his head shaved and gleaming under the lights. He was wearing a wife beater undershirt that shoved off his heavily muscled torso. He also had on khaki cargo shorts, ankle socks, and sneakers.

Rocco stayed on his tail until the man turned off Duval

and cut over to Caroline Street. Somewhere on Caroline Street, he lost the man in the shadows. Rocco hated that. But, he would call Marlow in the morning and tell him about it. Rocco started back towards his bike. He was stunned when something struck him in the back of the head and everything went black.

Lola decided to spend the night with Walter at the hospital. So, Marlow and Tina went back to his apartment, and Thom went home to his house on Big Coppitt Key.

"You are very worried about Walter, aren't you?" Tina asked.

"You know I am," Marlow sighed.

"You knew that he wouldn't live forever," Tina reminded him.

"I just didn't think it would be this soon. Walter is the closest thing I have to family besides you," Marlow said.

"You have Thom, as well," Tina prompted him.

"Thom is a good friend, but it just isn't the same."

"I know that. So, does Thom. You need to make your peace with this, Rick."

"I know that, Tina. It just isn't easy."

"I know that too, Ricky."

~ ~ ~

Marcus Dawes looked down at the kid he had knocked out. He didn't like being followed. He had no idea who the kid was which was why he had led him in the opposite direction from where he was really staying on Key Weird. He stomped on his right arm hearing the bone crack. That should send the message that he wanted to send. Then Dawes headed back to the house where he was staying, not giving the kid another thought.

~ ~ ~

Patrol Officer, Lucy Kincaid, spotted the kid on the sidewalk and turned on the searchlight on her patrol car and aimed at the crumpled form on the sidewalk. She radioed for back up before climbing out of the car, one hand on the butt of her service weapon as she approached. She could hear a soft moaning coming from the body, so she was pretty sure that he was still alive. "Are you okay?" she called. Another patrol car was coming from the other end of the street, mars lights flashing but without siren. It gave Lucy courage to move closer. It was a boy, or rather young man in late teens or early twenties. His face was familiar, and she knew that she had seen him around.

She also noted that his left arm was at an odd angle and swelling. There was some blood on the sidewalk that had dripped down from a head wound, too. She used her radio and called for a bus to the cross street where she had found him. It didn't take long to hear the drone of the sirens as the ambulance approached.

~ ~ ~

Tina had finally persuaded Marlow to go home. She had poured them both a tumbler of straight vodka. It was risk, one that could plunge Marlow back into a sea of drunkenness and despair. He had beat the bottle once, she hoped that he wouldn't have to try it again.

He had told her about his past, about losing his father. And then, being set up and shot and left for dead in an alley in New York facing charges of corruption before fleeing to Key West where he had tried to drink and smoke himself to death. Then, he had gone to work for Walter and had started getting himself straight. A cop named Della Martin had helped him quit smoking before killing herself. He had stopped smoking for good after that. Then, he had walked into her life and saved her. Now it was her turn to help save his.

Walter had been Marlow's father's best friend and he had taken an interest in Marlow, giving him a job and acting as his mentor to guide his career as a budding private investigator. He had, in effect, become a second father to the man she loved. Losing Walter would be catastrophic for Ricky. She wasn't sure that it wouldn't tip him over the edge. She would call Jessica back in the morning and have her come over to talk to him. He had done it for her. So, it was the least that she could do for him.

Tina carried the two drinks to the living room and sat one on the table in front of Marlow and held on to her own as she curled up on the couch next to him. "Do you want to talk about it?" Tina asked softly.

"Talking is sometimes very overrated," Marlow replied, as he took his first drink.

"Except when it's not," Tina countered, taking a sip of her own. The vodka was hot on her tongue, even though it was chilled from being in the freezer.

"Except when it's not," Marlow agreed.

"There is more to it than that, Ricky. You may not want to admit it, but there is."

"Maybe. It's this case, Tina. Quinn Kerns was here because she had been molested at home by her own father. Then, she made the mistake of trusting somebody she met here and then she disappeared. God only knows what sort of hell that she is being put through," Marlow sighed.

"You will find her, Rick. What she is going through is not your fault," Tina told him.

"I know that, but I'm not making any progress," Marlow shook his head.

"You will. You just have to do what you do best. Get out there and rattle cages and see what shakes loose. That's what you do. Go annoy people and see who reacts to it."

"I can do that," Marlow nodded. "How did you become so wise?"

"I listen and learn," Tina smiled at him.

"I think I need to go to bed," Marlow said, tossing the vodka back and putting the glass on the coffee table. He stood and moved to the bedroom. Tina finished her drink and left the glass on the table as she followed Marlow to bed, wishing that she could do more for him.

~ ~ ~

Walter Loomis made it through the night and Lola followed the ambulance to Miami General Hospital. She called Marlow from the road to give him the news. He told her that he would keep Walter's office closed and let clients know that Walter would be out of town for a few days.

Marlow broke the connection and poured himself a cup of coffee. He had already taken his morning run, showered and dressed. He had just started heating up coconut oil in a pan and broke three eggs into it, adding some cubed ham and chunks of jack cheese and some chopped green pepper into it. Tina appeared in the kitchen, still wearing her short silk kimono robe belted around her tiny waist. She had at least brushed her hair into some semblance of order and walked over and poured a cup of coffee before taking her seat at the table. Misty rubbed against her legs.

"Who was on the phone?" Tina asked after taking a sip of coffee.

"That was Lola. Walter made it through the night and they are transporting him to Miami. Lola is going with him," Marlow explained.

"What about the office?"

"It will be closed until Walter returns. I'll be calling and canceling his appointments."

"Are you sure that is the right thing to do?"

"What do you mean?"

"Ricky, there is a chance Walter will not be able to practice again. Shouldn't you tell his clients the truth?"

"What is he can though? It's not my call to make," Marlow told her.

"Then what are you going to do?" Tina asked.

"I'll leave it up to Walter and Lola. One thing I will do today is go see Hiram Shapiro as Walter asked for me to do."

"I think that is a good idea."

"First though, I'm taking you to work, just to be on the safe side."

"Thank you, Rick. I just don't feel safe out in the open."

"I know that, Tina. I will protect you," Marlow told her.

"I know that, Ricky. It doesn't make it any easier though," Tina told him.

"I know that too, kid," Marlow told her.

"I want you to talk to Jessica today."

"I can do that."

"I think you need to."

"I do, too," Marlow told her.

Chapter Fourteen

Marlow drove Tina to work and waited until she was safely inside the restaurant before pulling away and heading for Walter's office. He had several calls to make before going to see Hiram Shapiro. Most of them were to cancel Walter's appointments. One was to Sam Decker. He wanted Decker to dig deeper into Kurt Dawes' background. If Tina said she had seen him, he couldn't discount it. They knew that Dawes was a twin, but what if he was actually one of a set of identical triplets?

~ ~ ~

"Marlow, it's been a while," Sam Decker said, as he took a sip from the cold bottle of Killian's Red.

"I know it has, Sam. Tina and I were both sorry to hear about Lacy. I was away on a case for the funeral or we would have come up," Marlow told him.

"I figured, Rick. It's not a big deal. What can I do for you?"

"I was wondering if I could get you to look in on the background of guy named Kurt Dawes."

"Isn't that the guy that was stalking Tina a few months back?" Decker asked.

"Yeah, I shot and killed him. Tina just came back from Chicago testifying against his twin brother who was immediately locked up. Yet, since she's been back, she says she has seen Dawes twice," Marlow explained.

"Interesting. So, you want me to see if maybe the Dawes brothers were not just twins but triplets?"

"You got it."

"I can do that. You owe me a case of Killian's Red for my troubles," Decker told him.

"Deal," Marlow said before hanging up.

~ ~ ~

"Come to 'The Chart Room Bar', I'll be having lunch with Hiram Shapiro," Thom Hark told Marlow when he called.

"And who is paying for the lunch?" Marlow asked, already knowing the answer.

"You are, Ricky. After all, I am providing the introduction," Thom chuckled.

"Of course," Marlow growled before hanging up. He locked up the office and climbed into his car. He cracked the window until the air conditioner started blowing cold air and then he rolled it up. He drove to the pier where the 'Chart Room Bar' was located. He had no doubt that Thom and Shapiro were already inside.

It didn't take long for him to spot Thom and he made his way to the corner table where the two men sat waiting. Thom had a Bud Light sitting on the table in front of him and Shapiro was drinking a martini. Marlow dropped into an unoccupied chair and looked at the two men.

A waitress came by and Marlow ordered a Killian's Red. Once she left, he looked at the man that he took to be Hiram Shapiro. "Are you Hiram Shapiro?" Marlow asked.

"I am. I assume that you are Richard Marlow?"

"I am. You are Walter's attorney?"

"Yes. How is Walter?" Shapiro inquired.

"Stable, but they transferred him to Miami earlier this morning," Marlow said. "Lola went with him."

"I'm not surprised by that. They love each other a lot," Shapiro nodded.

"Yes, they do. So, why did Walter want me to come and see you?"

"I would rather have that discussion in my office, say about three o'clock?" Shapiro studied him.

"Three is good."

"I'll see you then, Shapiro said, standing and then he left Marlow and Thom Hark alone.

"What was that all about?" Marlow asked.

"I believe that he wanted to take your measure," Thom replied.

"Did I pass inspection?" Marlow asked.

"Apparently so, since he wants you to come to his office," Thom replied.

"Swell. Have you heard anything about Quinn Kerns?" Marlow asked.

"Not a word. I'm getting ready to break the story about her disappearance. Perhaps that will garner a lead or two," Thom espoused.

"We can only hope," Marlow agreed.

~ ~ ~

Marlow headed back to the office. Tina was working until five that afternoon. So, he would have plenty of time to meet with Shapiro before picking her up. He had a couple of cops that he needed to run background checks on. Maybe, he could figure out who on the force was actually a serial killer in disguise. Marlow drove out of the parking lot for the 'Pier House Resort' and headed back to his office. He was about halfway there when he noticed that he had a cop car on his tail. Marlow glanced at the speedometer. He was going the legal limit.

Marlow pulled over to the curb and waited. The cop car would either stop, or it would go on past. The car drove past, but not without the cop giving him a once over. The guy looked familiar, but the KWPD baseball cap and mirror lensed aviator style sunglasses kept Marlow from being able to positively identify him. Marlow wondered if it was one of the cops on the list that Sharp had given him. He pulled back out into traffic and kept an eye out for any police cars in his vicinity.

~ ~ ~

The message light was blinking on his answering machine when he unlocked and entered his office. Marlow punched in the code to disable the alarm before heading for his desk. He booted up his computer and played back the messages while he waited on it.

"Hey, Marlow. Rocco here. I saw some dude coming out of Tina's place last night and tried to follow him. Then, I got jumped and got the hell beat out of me. I'm at Lower Keys Medical Center," Rocco's voice told him. Marlow scooped up the phone and dialed the number for the medical center.

"My name is Rick Marlow. I'm calling to check on one of your patients. A young man named Rocco?" Marlow said when the phone was picked up at the other end.

"He had been hoping that you would call," the voice said. "Hang on a minute and I'll transfer you to his room."

"Sure thing," Marlow replied.

"Hello?" Rocco's voice sounded on the line.

"Rocco, are you okay? Your message said you got beat up," Marlow said.

"Yeah, I'm not exactly proud of that. Apparently, the guy that I was following spotted me and ambushed me. He knocked me out and then broke my arm by stomping on it," Rocco sighed.

"What did he look like?" Marlow asked, grabbing a post-it note so he could copy the description.

"He looked like the fucking Incredible Hulk except he wasn't green. I mean, fuck, his muscles had muscles! His head was bald, and he did his best to keep his face in the shadows, but he looked like that guy that had been stalking Tina a while back. But you shot that guy, right?" Rocco asked.

"I did. This guy might be one of his brothers," Marlow explained.

"Shit, that really sucks. Anyway, he knows where Tina lives. I saw him coming out of her apartment, and that's why I followed him," Rocco explained.

"You did good, Rocco. Don't worry about your hospital bills, I'll cover them," Marlow told him before hanging up. Another Kurt Dawes? It was looking more and more like the guy was triplets!

Marlow opened up his browser and typed in the address of one of the many data bases that were available to private eyes and law enforcement. He entered the names of the cops on the list that Sharp had given him and sat back to let the computer do the work.

~ ~ ~

Oscar had been surprised when Marlow had spotted

him after leaving the restaurant. He hadn't counted on that. So, he had driven past giving Marlow the once over. He was pretty sure that the P.I. hadn't recognized him, but he couldn't be a hundred per cent sure.

He decided that he would give the guy some space and see where he went. Right now, it looked like Marlow was headed back to Walter Loomis's house where he had an office. It would be easy enough to pick him up there later.

~ ~ ~

"Where am I?" Walter Loomis asked as he opened his eyes to see Lola Ponsberry looking down at him."

"Miami General Hospital. You had another heart attack," Lola explained.

"Then, I obviously survived it," Walter said weakly.

"Just barely. They had to restart your heart three times," Lola told him.

"Perhaps," Walter said, "it is time for me to retire."

"Yes, yes, it is," Lola told him.

"Have Ricky contact Hiram Shapiro."

"He already has. He's meeting him in his office at three this afternoon," Lola told him.

"Good. Hiram will take care of you both," Walter said.

"Walter," Lola said.

"Don't argue with me, Lola. I honestly don't know how much time I have left. But, will you marry me?" Walter asked.

"I will," Lola told him.

"Thank you for making an old man happy. Can you send for a preacher?" Walter asked.

"Yes, sweetheart," Lola told him, tears streaming down her cheeks.

"Thank you," Walter told her. Lola hit the call button and as soon as the nurse entered the doorway, she requested that the hospital send her the hospital chaplain. Lola squeezed Walter's hands.

"I hope that you don't mind," Walter said to her.

"I couldn't be happier," Lola responded with a smile.

~ ~ ~

Hiram Shapiro looked up when his secretary opened the door and ushered Rick Marlow inside his office. Marlow was still wearing an aloha shirt over a wife beater ribbed tank top, and khaki cargo shorts and white New Balance walking shoes. His wavy brown hair was combed back from his face. Walter had told him that Marlow usually wore a stainless steel snub-nosed .38 caliber revolver in a clip on holster on his right hip.

"How is Walter doing?" Shapiro asked.

"The last I heard, he had made it through the night and was being transferred to Miami General Hospital," Marlow replied.

"That sounds hopeful. I assume you are here because he asked you to come and talk to me?"

"You would be correct," Marlow admitted.

"Walter had me make certain arrangements so that you and Lola would be well taken care of if anything happened to him. This being his second major heart attack, he apparently felt that it was time to make you aware of the arrangements," Shapiro explained.

Marlow looked at the thick folder on the desk top in front of Shapiro. "Does that contain the arrangements?"

"It does. So, do you want to hear them?"

"It doesn't seem like I have much choice," Marlow

sighed.

"There is always a choice. You could wait to see if he pulls through."

"No, he wouldn't have wanted me to come if he didn't feel that I should know immediately."

"Well, we do agree on that. I checked you out, Marlow. Thom Hark and Chief Gutierrez both speak as highly of you, just as Walter did."

"Glad to hear it," Marlow sighed.

"So, let's get started," Shapiro said, as he opened the folder and pulled out the thick sheath of papers it contained.

~ ~ ~

"I now pronounce you husband and wife. Mr. Loomis, you may kiss your bride," Chaplain Peter York told them.

"Gladly," Walter said, leaning forward in the bed to kiss Lola on the mouth. Once they broke the kiss, Lola was beaming as was her new husband. The two nurses that had served as witnesses signed the marriage license that the chaplain had brought with him. He promised that it would be taken to the courthouse and registered, and then returned to them before the day was out.

"Thank you, Father," Walter told him. You just made us both the happiest people on earth."

"It was my pleasure," Chaplain York told them.

~ ~ ~

Tina was wiping down a table when she got the feeling that she was being watched. It was a creepy feeling and sent chills down her spine. She looked up and scanned the inside of Pepe's. None of the customers was watching her. She looked outside. Kurt Dawes was standing outside looking in through the window. He looked even bigger than she remembered. When he saw that she had spotted him, he made a gun with his finger and thumb, and pointed at her. He smiled and then took off. Tina couldn't help it. She fainted.

Chapter Fifteen

Marlow had just left Hiram Shapiro's office when his cell phone rang. "Marlow," he answered.

"Marlow, this is Juan, Tina just collapsed here at work. I've got an ambulance on the way," Tina's boss told him.

"I'm on my way too," Marlow said, hanging up and running for his car. He tossed his phone into the passenger seat and cranked the engine of the Ford Focus to life. Shifting to drive, he pulled away from the curb in a squeal of burning rubber.

What could have caused Tina to collapse? Had something happened in Chicago that she was just now having a reaction to? Or had Kurt Dawes found a way to strike at her from the grave? Marlow shivered at the thought but couldn't dismiss it. Not after some of the shit he had seen since coming to Key West.

Marlow arrived at the same time as the ambulance. He was inside right behind the EMT's who were kneeling next to Tina. Juan or one of the girls had put towels under the back of her next to keep her breathing passages open and had turned her head to the side to make sure that if she vomited that she would be able to aspirate it. Marlow dropped to his knees beside her, trying to stay out of the way the EMT's. "Tina, can you hear me, baby?" Marlow asked, his voice cracking with emotion.

"Her vitals are good," the EMT said, digging in his bag. He brought out a glass ampoule of smelling salts and broke it open and waved it under Tina's nose. Her whole body jerked as she tried to sit up, her eyes snapping open. She spotted Marlow right away.

"Ricky, what are you doing here?" she asked groggily.

"I think she'll be okay. But if she has any other problems, get her to a doctor right away," the EMT told Marlow as he stood.

"Will do," Marlow told him before returning his attention to Tina. "You collapsed, and Juan called me right after he called the ambulance. Do you remember what happened?"

"I had a feeling like that I was being watched. I turned around and Kurt Dawes was looking through the window at me. After that, everything went blank," Tina shook her head.

"Baby, I shot and killed Kurt Dawes two years ago," Marlow told her.

"Dammit, Rick. I saw him!"

"Okay, I believe you," Marlow said softly, doing his best to comfort her.

"I hope so," Tina sighed, leaning into him.

"You go home and get some rest. Take tomorrow off, too," Juan told her.

"Are you sure?" Tina looked at her boss.

'You're the best waitress I have. I need you at your best," Juan told her with a smile.

"Okay," Tina agreed. She went and clocked out,

pocketing her tips for the day and Marlow escorted her to his car. He got her inside it and drove home to his apartment. They had just got inside when his cell phone rang again. It was Sam Decker calling.

"Hey, Sam," Marlow answered.

"Your hunch paid off, pal. Kurt Dawes was one of triplets. His brothers are Jason and Marcus. Jason is currently residing in Illinois State Prison, but Marcus appears to have dropped out of sight," Decker told him.

"Sam, could I get you to come down and watch over Tina for a few days?"

"How about I send Rafael? I've got to get Mark enrolled in school and take care of some family stuff."

"That will work. Take care of yourself, Sam."

"You too, Rick," Decker told him before hanging up.

"What was that all about?" Tina asked.

"Rafael Cortez is going to come down and hang out with you until we get this mess cleaned up. Don't bother arguing," Marlow told her.

"I'm too scared to argue at this point," Tina whispered.

"I know, honey, and I hate that. Rafael is good people and he'll take care of you just like you were family," Marlow told her.

"I hope you are right," Tina sighed.

"I am. Right now, I'm going to find Marcus Dawes and I'll put him in the ground just like I did his brother," Marlow told her, meaning it.

~ ~ ~

On their way back to Marlow's place, he called Jessica Harmon and asked her to come over explaining what had happened. "What about your other case, the missing girl?"

Tina asked as he drove.

"I may have something on that. At first, we thought the sketch was Steve Lorca, but then Sharp noticed that it also looked like a few guys on the police force and had me run background checks on them. It seems that there is one that doesn't appear to have existed farther back than seven years ago," Marlow explained.

"That sounds promising," Tina nodded.

"It does. Problem is how to check him out closer without tipping him off that we are looking into him. According to his personnel file, he has a mentally challenged brother that lives with him."

"So, a helper then?"

"Possibly. I need to call Sharp and see how she wants to approach this, but I won't do that until Rafael arrives to stay with you."

"Ricky, once Jessica gets there I will be fine. You know she packs a gun and knows how to use it," Tina rolled her eyes.

"Maybe I don't want to have her have to use it? It was hard enough on her when she had to shoot at the former mayor when he was trying to get to Lilly Brisbane. I don't want to have to put her through that again."

"You have a big heart, Ricky. How is Walter doing?" Tina asked.

"So far, so good. He and Lola got married at the hospital this morning. Lola called to tell me the news," Marlow explained.

"Oh, I am so happy for them both," Tina smiled. Marlow was glad to see the smile. It wasn't something that he had seen much of since she had returned from Chicago.

"I am, too. Though I have a feeling that there are going to be a lot of changes in the immediate future," Marlow sighed.

"What do you mean?"

"I met with Hiram Shapiro earlier today."

"Who is that?" Tina looked puzzled.

"Walter's attorney. If anything happens to Walter, I inherit his house. There is more. If Lola wants to stay on, she will be my secretary until such a time as one or the other of us dies."

"Wow, that's pretty heavy."

"It is. Also, Walter has divided his assets between Lola and I evenly and they are not an inconsiderable sum. I had no idea," Marlow shook his head.

"I can't say I am surprised. Walter has always treated you both like family. It's only natural that he would leave it to you both after his own daughters tried to kill him," Tina said.

"I guess I'm just not all that sure I am comfortable with it," Marlow sighed as he pulled up in front of his duplex. He put the car in park and shut off the engine.

"Ricky, I know you love Walter like a second father. He was there for you after your own father was killed in the line of duty. It can't be easy for you to think about him possibly dying," Tina told him.

"It's not. I've always looked at Walter as being indestructible. He has always had a sense of permanence about him, like a statue. Seeing him in the hospital last night, well, it reminded me of my own mortality. It shook me to the core," Marlow explained.

"It would shake anyone."

"Maybe, but I have my doubts."

"I believe in you, Ricky, you should too," Tina told him.

"I'm trying, Tina. I'm trying," Marlow told her. They climbed out of the car and made their way to the front door of the house. Marlow unlocked the door and they went inside and headed up the stairs.

~ ~ ~

Evelyn Sharp rubbed her eyes. She was tired. She was waiting for Marlow to get back to her with his results of the background checks. Evelyn stood and headed for the chief's office. She figured that he needed to know what she had found.

"Hello, Detective Sharp, what can I do for you?" Chief Gutierrez asked her when she knocked on the door to his office.

"I've got some news."

"Glad to hear it. I could use some good news for a change."

"Yes, I can understand that."

"So, what have you got for me?"

"Nothing good, chief," Sharp said, closing the door behind her.

~ ~ ~

Marcus Dawes frowned as he sat down in his rented room. The house was owned by a little old lady and he was just one of four renters. The room contained a bed, a closet, a dresser, and a beat-up television. His suitcase was stored in the closet along with half a dozen fake id's and four envelopes containing a thousand dollars in small bills. Once he had taken care of that stupid bitch that had got one of his brothers killed and another sent to prison, he planned to head for Mexico and disappear there and never come back to the States.

He opened one of the drawers in the dresser and removed a bottle of Jack Daniels and a small glass. He poured two fingers full and recapped the bottle before taking a sip. It burned going down, but it was a smooth burn that he almost didn't notice until he felt the explosion of warmth in his stomach.

Marcus had gone to his brother's trial, but he had worn a disguise and stayed at the back of the courtroom. He had gotten a good look at Tina Cord, but she had never even noticed him. She would never have given Kurt a second look if she hadn't walked up on him raping that girl in the alley. Old Kurt could really hold a grudge, he thought with a smile. His brother knew how to pick 'em. Kurt had chased Tina Cord and almost had her when Tina's new boyfriend had shot and killed him as he was just about to finally exact his revenge on her. Marcus drained the rest of the whiskey and walked to the bathroom to rinse out the glass. He wiped it dry with a clean washcloth and carried it back and put it in the drawer with the bottle. Then, he lay back on the bed and started to plan his next steps.

~ ~ ~

"I want you to go back to Key West, Lola. As much as I love Ricky, he can't keep the office running by himself, especially when he's the only one there," Walter told his new bride.

"Are you sure, Walter?" Lola held his hand tightly in hers. She had never seen him look so frail.

"I'm sure, my love. If you like, wait and see what the doctor says, but I am sure that he'll have me up and around in no time at all."

"Are you sure?"

"I am. But please, speak with my doctor first."

"I will," Lola promised him.

"I really will be okay, Lola. We just got married, and I, at least, plan to have a honeymoon with you," Walter said pointedly. Lola blushed furiously.

"Not until the doctor says you are healthy enough for sex, dear husband!" Lola said primly.

"Well, it had better be soon," Walter grinned at her.

"Walter!" Lola said, acting shocked. Then she began to smile as well.

~ ~ ~

Marlow had gotten Tina home and he waited at the door until Jessica Harmon arrived and he led her upstairs. She and Tina hugged right away. "How are you, Tina? Marlow told me what happened!" Jessica told her.

"I don't know how, but one of the Dawes brothers is back on the island," Tina was close to tears. Jessica looked over at Marlow for confirmation.

"Kurt Dawes wasn't just a twin he was one of three identical triplets," Marlow explained.

"So, who is here on the island?" Jessica looked puzzled.

"As near as I have been able to find out, the third brother, Marcus," Marlow explained.

"And the hits just keep on coming," Jess said, shaking her head.

"They do, but we have to help her through this."

"I know that, Marlow," Jessica told him.

~ ~ ~

"So, you are telling me I may have a serial killer on my

force?" Chief Gutierrez asked his eyes wide with shock.

"I said it is possible, but not definite," Detective Sharp told him.

"This is not a good thing," Gutierrez shook his head.

"No, it's not. I don't have confirmation yet. Marlow is running checks on the officers that I think may be involved.

Chapter Sixteen

"Jessica, thanks for coming over," Marlow said as he greeted the psychiatrist when he answered the door.

"Not a problem, I didn't have any patients today," Jessica Harmon replied. "How is Tina?"

"She's almost in as bad a shape as Lilly Brisbane was. She saw one of the Dawes brothers, apparently an identical triplet that we knew nothing about until I had Sam Decker dig into the Dawes family. His partner, Rafael Cortez, is on the way to keep Tina safe while I continue to hunt for Quinn Kerns," Marlow explained.

"That sounds like a step in the right direction. I'll hang out with her too and try to keep her from retreating into deep depression."

"Thank you, Jessica.

"It's what I do, Rick."

"No, you've gone above and beyond to help us. I want you to know how much I appreciate it," Marlow told her. Jessica reached up and patted his shoulder before moving around him and heading up the stairs. His phone picked that moment to ring and he snatched it from his pocket. "Marlow," he said.

"It's Rafael, Marlow. Sam told me to give you a call once

I got on the island and get directions to the house," Rafael Cortez told him.

"Right. Thanks for coming down and helping me with this. Tina needs to be protected and I'm trying to find a missing girl that is in grave danger," Marlow explained.

"No problem. You can give me a rundown on this Dawes guy when I get there," Rafael said.

"Sounds good," Marlow said before hanging up. He locked the front door and climbed back up the stairs.

~ ~ ~

Jessica and Tina were sitting on the couch with fresh cups of coffee in front of them on the coffee table. Marlow walked past into the kitchen and poured himself a cup as well, adding some sugar before heading back out to take the chair next to the couch. Misty was curled up in Tina's lap purring contentedly. The sound seemed to be helping Tina relax which Marlow was glad for.

"That was Cortez, he'll be here soon. Once he gets here, I'm heading over to the police station to see what Sharp has found out about two possibly involved cops," Marlow explained.

"You don't have to worry, Rick. I know what Rafael looks like," Tina told him.

"That's not it, angel. I've got to fill him in about the Dawes brothers or, at least what I know. He'll probably have questions for you, as well," Marlow explained.

"Okay," Tina replied softly.

"Don't worry, Tina. I'll be right here beside you," Jessica told her. Tina nodded, not saying anything else. "Besides, I know what Rafael looks like, too," she looked pointedly at Marlow. It was then that he remembered that she had taken on both Sam and his ward, Mark, after Lacy Ryan's death and the death of Mark's father.

"Thank you again, Jess," Marlow told her. There was a knock on the door. "That should be Rafe," Marlow said, as he headed for the door. He walked down the steps, drawing his .38 as he did so. He opened the door and Rafael Cortez stood there looking like a young Antonio Banderas. Marlow holstered his gun and opened the door letting the Cuban P.I. inside. Marlow took him up and introduced him to Tina and then left to go and talk to Detective Sharp.

~ ~ ~

Rocco couldn't ride his bike with the broken arm. He was stuck walking wherever he went after being discharged from the Lower Keys Medical Center. He knew that Marlow had made arrangements to pay for his medical bills, not because he felt indebted to him, but because that was just the kind of guy that Marlow was.

Rocco wanted to find the asshole that had beat him down and broke his arm and get a little payback. Marlow would be against the idea and that was why he wasn't going to tell him. No, he owed that big son of a bitch plenty!

~ ~ ~

Evelyn Sharp looked up as Marlow entered the squad room. He looked worn and tired. It made her feel a little bit sorry for him. "What have you got?" he asked, as he dropped into the chair beside her desk.

"I've informed the chief and he wants us to keep working it. Have you narrowed it down any?" Sharp asked, brushing a stray lock of hair out of her face.

"I have. Patrolman Christopher James. Until seven years ago, he didn't even exist," Marlow explained.

"He's off tonight. Do you want to pay him a visit?"

"If we do, we are likely to tip him off," Marlow shook his head.

"I thought you wanted to find the girl," Sharp looked at him.

"I do, but I don't want to tip James off that we are looking at him."

"So, how do you want to pursue this?"

"According to his file, he has a brother with mental challenges."

"So?"

"So, we wait until James goes to work and then we go see the brother," Marlow explained.

"Attacking the weakest link, then?" Sharp asked.

"Something like that," Marlow nodded.

"Go talk to the chief. If he approves it, we will do it," Sharp told him. Marlow nodded, stood and headed to the chief's office.

~ ~ ~

Chief Jamie Gutierrez looked up as Marlow knocked on his open door before stepping inside. "I've been expecting you," Jamie told him.

"I figured. Detective Sharp told me that she had told you what I found out," Marlow said as he took the seat across from the chief of police. He had shut the door behind him when he entered.

"So, how are you going to play this?"

"I'm going to wait for James to go to work, and then I'm going to drop in on his brother. I have a feeling that he's the weak link in James's armor."

"I'm not sure that I like the idea of you going after a kid

that is mentally challenged. It doesn't feel right," Chief Gutierrez shook his head.

"I'm not happy about it either, but it may be Quinn Kerns only chance at coming out of this alive," Marlow sighed.

"You're positive James is the one that took her?"

"I am. He didn't even exist until seven years ago."

"Okay, do what you have to do but keep Sharp with you just to be on the safe side. According to the schedule, James reports for duty at four o'clock. Will that give you enough time?"

"It will have to," Marlow shrugged.

"What's this I hear about the ghost of Kurt Dawes returning to the island?" Gutierrez asked.

"Turns out he was one of identical triplets instead of twins. After I took out Dawes and Tina put one of the brothers in prison for pretending to be him while Kurt stalked her, Marcus Dawes has come to the island to settle accounts. Not to mention, Walter had another heart attack and is in Miami General Hospital," Marlow sighed.

"Sounds like you've got a hell of a lot on your plate," Jamie said.

"Almost too damn much," Marlow admitted.

"Who's taking care of Tina while you're on this other stuff?"

"Sam Decker sent Rafael Cortez down to watch over Tina while I hunt for Quinn."

"Oh, Jesus Christ, Marlow! Do you know who Cortez used to work for?" Jamie exploded.

"I do, but it has been a lot of years, Jamie. He and Decker are not partners in Decker's business, and they have been for a few years. I trust Rafael as much as I trust Sam," Marlow replied.

"Then get out of here and find Quinn Kerns. The sooner I have Rafael Cortez off my island, the happier I am going to be," Jamie sighed, putting his face in his hands.

Marlow nodded and stood, leaving. He headed back to Sharp's desk. She looked up at his approach. "He gave the okay," Marlow told her.

"Then, let's do this," Evelyn Sharp said, standing up and grabbing her jacket. She pulled it on as she followed Marlow to the elevator.

~ ~ ~

Rocco was haunting Duval Street looking for the big guy he had spotted coming out of Tina's apartment. He owed that son of a bitch for his concussion and the broken arm. Rocco wanted payback. He wasn't exactly sure how he was going to get it, but he could figure that part out later. Right now, he just wanted to find the guy!

~ ~ ~

Walter Loomis lay back on the bed. He was not feeling near as well as he had led Lola to believe. At least, now they were married. He owed her that much. He had loved her for as long as she loved him, but until Marlow had prompted him, he had never acted on it.

His time on earth was rapidly approaching its end. He realized it even if his doctor did not. He had spent much of the time since his last heart attack preparing for it. He had made arrangements for both Marlow and Lola so that even after he was dead, they would both be able to continue. That was part of why he had sent Lola back to Key West. He had not wanted her to see him die.

The end was coming. He knew it. He accepted it. Lola would be heartbroken, Marlow too. But they would both survive. He knew that they would both need each other once he was gone.

~ ~ ~

Officer Christopher James left his house heading for the station. There were days when he felt bad about leaving his little brother alone. But there was nothing that he could do about it. Besides, his brother did a good job of keeping things taken care of when he was gone.

~ ~ ~

"He's off to work," Marlow observed.

"Perhaps he is. But what if he's not?" Sharp asked.

"So, you want to wait?"

"I think that is a good idea."

"In case he circles back around?"

"Yep. Remember, even paranoid people are right sometimes."

"Touché," Marlow agreed.

~ ~ ~

Rafael made a circuit of Marlow's side of the duplex, checking every possible entrance and exit. He wanted a good read just in case this Dawes character made a try for Tina Cord at Marlow's place. He had found a couple of decent defensible positions if needed inside. He, also, set up an emergency rope ladder connected to the sill of the bedroom if worse came to worst. They had one extra area where they could escape. The ladders were often used for emergency escape routes in case of fire. Once he had the apartment secured, he headed back to where Tina and Dr. Harmon sat in the living room.

He knew Jessica, of course, from her work not only with Sam, but with Mark as well. "How is Mark doing?" Jessica asked, as Rafael sat down in the chair that was located to the side where he could see both them and the stairwell coming up from the front door. Rafael removed a 12-guage Mossberg Persuader shotgun from his duffle and laid it across his knees before answering.

"Mark is doing better. Sam got him a dog," Rafael replied.

"A dog? I thought Sam didn't like dogs," Jessica sounded shocked.

"Elvis didn't like dogs, but Elvis died," Rafael shrugged.

"Sam loved that cat, almost as much as he loved Lacy."

"It hit him hard. I think that's why he got Mark the dog to take away the sting of the loss. They both seem better now. Sam had to get Mark enrolled in the Scorpion Cay school today. Otherwise, he would have come himself," Rafael explained.

"When you see Sam, tell him I was sorry to hear about Elvis. He was a good kitty," Tina said.

"I will, and it will mean a lot to Sam and Mark both," Rafael replied.

"I hope so. Mark is a good kid," Tina replied.

"Both Mark and Sam, have gone through a lot in the last year," Jessica affirmed.

~ ~ ~

"It's been thirty minutes. James is at the station by now for roll call," Evelyn Sharp said.

"Now, it is time to go talk to his brother," Marlow said.

"Let's do this," Sharp said, opening her door and climbing out of the car. Together, they headed up the sidewalk to the front door.

Chapter Seventeen

Georgie was surprised when he heard the knock on the front door. Who could be knocking? Oscar left for work a long time ago and he always carried his key with him when he went out. Georgie scratched his head and headed for the door.

Georgie knew that Oscar would be mad about him opening the door, but what choice did he have? If he didn't answer the door, it would be rude. Georgie reached the front door and unlocked it and opened the big inside door. A man and woman were standing there. The woman was wearing a suit and she looked nice. The man looked like a beach bum. "Can I help you?" Georgie asked.

The woman held up a police badge. "We're Key West Police Detectives. We were wondering if we could speak to you," the lady detective smiled as she spoke. Georgie though that she had a very pretty smile.

"I guess so. My brother is a police officer too," Georgie said with a touch of pride.

"May we come in?" the lady asked.

"Uh, I don't think my brother would like that. But I can come outside and talk to you," Georgie said with a beaming smile. The beach bum gave the lady a nod and they both stepped back so that Georgie could step outside. He pulled the big door shut behind him. "So, what do you want to talk about?"

~ ~ ~

Marlow let Evelyn take the lead. Georgie responded to her in a way Marlow knew that the kid would never respond to him. So, he stepped back to let Sharp do the heavy lifting for the moment. He watched as she pulled out a picture of Quinn Kerns out of a pocket, keeping it out of Georgie's sight.

"We are looking for a missing girl. She was last seen right before the hurricane hit. Did you and your brother ride it out here?" Sharp asked.

"Yes, we did. This house was built strong," Georgie said with pride.

"You seem to know a lot about the houses around here. Have you seen any young women hanging around?" Sharp kept her eyes focused on his as she waited on an answer. Georgie looked down and to the left.

"Have you seen this girl?" Sharp showed him the picture of Quinn and his face lost all color.

"Uh . . . no," Georgie stammered.

"You're lying, Georgie," Marlow said, his voice hard and angry sounding. Georgie hunched his shoulder as if he were afraid of being hit.

"Tell us where Quinn is, Georgie," Sharp commanded quietly, her voice soft and soothing. Georgie started to cry, tears welling up in his eyes and streaming down his cheeks.

"Oscar is going to be so mad at me. He told me not to talk about Quinn, but he did things to her that hurt her. She always is nice to me," Georgie sobbed.

"Is she in the house?" Marlow asked softly. Georgie

nodded, still crying. Marlow opened the door and went inside taking the nod as permission to enter and search the premises.

Once inside, Marlow drew his .38 and moved from room to room until he found a locked door. Marlow rapped on the door. "Hello? Is anybody in there?" He heard a weak cry for help from behind the door. Lifting his right foot, Marlow drove it against the door right below the latch. The door flew open, but the room was dark. Marlow stepped inside feeling around for the light switch. When he found it, he turned the lights on.

There was a naked girl tied to the bed. She had long light brown hair and pale blue eyes. Her nude body had been abused a lot, but she was still alive and frightened. Marlow holstered his gun and knelt by the bed drawing a knife and opening it so that he could cut her loose. Once that was done, Marlow found a blanket to cover her with and helped her out the front door to Detective Sharp's car.

Sharp had cuffs on Georgie and had him sitting on the front porch. "Do you want me to call Jamie?" Marlow asked her.

"Yes, have him pick up Christopher James," Sharp said sadly. She had hoped that the kidnapper had not been a cop.

"Will do," Marlow said as he pulled out his phone and dialed. When the chief answered, Marlow told him, "We got her. She's alive. Get Christopher James in custody."

"I'm on it," Chief Gutierrez replied. He checked his watch. James should still have been in roll call. He hurried to the elevator stabbing the button for the ground floor.

~ ~ ~

Marlow had also called an ambulance for Quinn. It took

a few minutes, but finally they could see the ambulance turning down the street. Marlow dialed the number for Quinn's mother so that he could let her know that he had found her daughter. He suspected that, given what she had been through, they would transfer her to Miami General which was better equipped to deal with her level of trauma than the Lower Keys Medical Center.

~ ~ ~

The chief entered the roll call room just as the duty officer for the afternoon shift was getting ready to dismiss his men. When the chief entered, the officers all snapped to attention. "Chief, what can I do for you?" Captain Mulder asked.

"I need to speak to Patrolman Christopher James," Chief Gutierrez said loudly. "Where is he, please?"

"Here, Sir," James said, looking puzzled.

"Officers Pike and Keaton. Please, put Officer James in cuffs and relieve him of his weapon," the chief ordered. James started to fight and protest, but the two larger officers made short work of him. Soon, they were leading him to booking.

The shift supervisor walked over. "Care to let me in on what the hell is going on?" Captain Mulder asked.

"It will come out soon enough. Patrolman James was responsible for the kidnapping and imprisonment of a juvenile runaway that came here right before Irma tore through. Detective Sharp found the girl chained to a bed in his home just shortly before I came down and had him arrested," Chief Gutierrez replied.

"I'll put in the paperwork for him to be fired," Mulder said, looking angry.

"The sooner the better," the chief replied, heading back to his office.

~ ~ ~

Marcus Dawes sat in his car parked halfway down the block from Rick Marlow's apartment. He wondered about the dusty black Dodge Charger. He hadn't seen it before. He wondered where Marlow was. Marcus wanted to kill him, as well as Tina Cord. It had been the pair of them that had taken his brothers away from him. Killing one wouldn't satisfy him. No, they *both* had to die!

~ ~ ~

Marlow rode in the ambulance with Quinn Kerns to the Lower Keys Medical Center where she would be evaluated. Sharp had cuffed Georgie and put him in her car to take back to the station. The county CSI unit was on the way to the house and there were two uniforms on the scene stringing crime scene tape around the house.

Quinn looked up at him with a look of admiration. Marlow patted her hand and murmured comforting words to her to keep her calm as the ambulance covered the distance to the medical center. Once there, after Quinn had been taken inside, Marlow pulled out his cell phone and dialed Mrs. Kerns' number.

"Hello?" she answered. Her voice sounded shaky.

"Mrs. Kerns, this is Rick Marlow. I'm with your daughter, Quinn, at the Lower Keys Medical Center. I found her," Marlow told her.

"Thank you, Mr. Marlow, thank you so much!" Mrs. Kerns was openly sobbing now. Marlow could tell that they were tears of joy that her daughter had been found alive.

"We will wait here for you to arrive," Marlow told her

before hanging up.

~ ~ ~

Officer Christopher James chaffed as he worked his hands in the cuffs that kept him bolted to the table in the interrogation room. Georgie must have fucked up somehow. It was the only explanation. He had held onto Quinn Kerns for too long. Especially, after finding out that somebody was looking for her. He should have killed her the night that he first spotted Marlow putting up the flyers and then took her out into the Gulf and dumped her in for the sharks.

Instead, he had kept her too long, played with her too long. And now, he was arrested and probably going to get the death penalty if convicted. His real name was Oscar Christopher James, but he never used his first name because he hated it. If he discovered any opportunity, he would escape, and he would seek revenge not only on Quinn Kerns, but on whoever had helped her.

~ ~ ~

Lola Ponsberry sat at the reception desk at the office. Marlow was out, and she wasn't sure exactly why her husband had sent her back to the office. So far, all she had done was field calls from clients who were calling to wish Walter well. Life was going on, despite Walter not being there. She wondered if it would continue that way once he announced that he was retiring.

Lola knew that some of his clients would not take the news well, but there was little she could do about that. She would just have to do her best to shield him from angry clients once he was back home. It was the least that she could do.

She picked up the telephone and dialed Marlow's cell number, waiting as it started to ring. "Marlow," he finally answered.

"I'm at the office if you need me. Walter sent me home to be of assistance if you needed me," Lola told him.

"I appreciate that, Lola. I found Quinn Kerns and I'm now at the Lower Keys Medical Center with her while she is being examined," Marlow explained.

"I'll call Walter and let him know. I'm sure he will be pleased," Lola replied.

"I think so, too," Marlow told her. "So, how is Walter doing?"

"According to the doctor, he is doing okay, but Rick . . . I'm not so sure," Lola told him.

"Why is that?"

"It's just a feeling really. I think that Walter is not telling me everything," Lola admitted.

"He rarely does," Marlow admitted.

"So, what do we do now?" Lola asked.

"I'll call his doctor, Lola," Marlow promised her.

~ ~ ~

Marlow leaned back against the cinderblock wall. It had been a long day. He dialed Thom Hark and waited for the newspaperman to answer. "Marlow, my boy, what is going on?" Hark asked.

"I found Quinn Kerns. Patrol Officer Christopher James had kidnapped her and was using her as a sex slave since before Irma hit the island," Marlow told him.

"Is the girl okay?" Thom asked.

"She's as good as she can be after what she went through. You might head over to the police station and see what you can get for the newspaper," Marlow told him.

"I'm on my way," Thom told him.

~ ~ ~

Tina Cord had gone to the bedroom to take a nap. Jessica and Rafael were keeping one eye on her and one on the stairs. "When do you think Dawes might come for her?" Jessica asked.

"I wish I knew," Rafael shrugged.

"I think it will be soon. Tina is responsible for the death and imprisonment of both of his brothers. A man like Marcus Dawes cannot let something like that go," Jessica replied.

"You are right, he can't. I figure by now, he's spotted my car and is wondering about it. I want to keep him wondering," Rafael shrugged.

"Why is that?" Jessica asked.

"Because it keeps Dawes off balance. It is a variable that he hasn't been able to figure out ahead of time."

"You seem sure of that," Jessica observed.

"Because I am. This is not my first rodeo," Rafael told her.

"I suppose not. I know that Ricky trusts you. I suppose I should, too," Jessica sighed.

"Yes, you should," he told her.

~ ~ ~

Christopher James looked up as Detective Evelyn Sharp entered the interrogation room. She looked cool and composed in her grey slacks and jacket. "Hello, Officer James," she said.

"What the hell is going on?" James asked.

"Georgie already spilled the beans, Oscar. He told us all about Quinn and the other girls," Sharp told him.

Chapter Eighteen

"**W**ell shit," Oscar James sighed. "Georgie was always my weakness. My little brother that my mom made me take care of him while she was out getting her drugs. After she left, I just did it. I could have dumped him some place, but family is family, you know?"

"Talk to me about Quinn Kerns, Oscar," Sharp prodded him.

"I want my union rep," James looked up at her coldly.

"You've been fired, Mr. James. You are no longer entitled to union representation. You're facing multiple charges ranging from kidnapping, illegal detention of a minor, multiple counts of rape of a minor. As well as numerous other charges," Sharp told him.

"Then I want a lawyer and I refuse to say another word until I've met with counsel," James smirked.

"If that's the way you want it," Sharp stood and walked out of the room. Two other officers came in, unhooked him from the table and walked him back to the holding cell where he would await transport to the county jail by the sheriff's department.

It worried him that he didn't see Georgie anywhere. If Georgie was telling all like the detective had said, James knew that he would be looking at hard time and possibly the death penalty.

He had to figure a way to get out of here to shut his little brother up once and for all. That thought nearly broke his heart. He had always taken care of his little brother. But this time, he needed to save his own ass. If that meant Georgie had to die, then Georgie had to die!

~ ~ ~

Marlow was in the waiting room at the Lower Keys Medical Center when Marla Kerns rushed in from the street. "How is she, Mr. Marlow?" Marla Kerns asked.

"The doctors are in with her now and they say, while she's in rough shape physically, she should recover. But she's going to need psychiatric help, as well. I can recommend a doctor if you like. She specializes in post-traumatic stress syndrome. Her name is Jessica Harmon and her offices are right here on the island," Marlow told her.

"I agree, Mr. Marlow. I know a thing or two about rape that you'll never know, that you can never know because you aren't a woman. I'll make sure that Quinn gets the help she needs," Marla told him. Marlow nodded and stood.

"Since you are here for Quinn, I'm going to go," Marlow told her.

"I appreciate it, Mr. Marlow. I'll be fine, thanks to you. So will Quinn," Marla smiled.

Marlow gave her a smile and nodded before heading outside. Once out in the evening air, he immediately started to sweat as he pulled out his cell phone and dialed up a taxi to take him back to the police station to get his car. He sent Tina a text to see how she was doing. And to let her know that he had found Quinn and that the girl was still alive.

~ ~ ~

Marcus Dawes had given up watching Marlow's place had headed back across town to where Tina Cord had her apartment. He had gotten inside a couple of times without trouble. A third time would be just as easy. Only this time, he was going to leave a big surprise for her when she finally came home. One that, if all went well, she wouldn't survive!

~ ~ ~

The taxi took Marlow back to the office where he was surprised to find Lola hard at work. "What are you still doing here?" he asked as he entered the reception area.

"Last time I looked, I still work here," Lola replied.

"How is Walter?" he asked, suddenly concerned.

"This is my husband's idea. He said you would likely need my help and that the hospital would likely release him in a couple of days."

"Congrats on the wedding, Lola. Yes, I know how stubborn Walter can be. He has always hated having people make a fuss over him."

"That is very true."

"So, I found Quinn Kerns today. It turns out, a rogue cop had taken her and was keeping her as a sex slave. It, also, appears that she wasn't the first young woman that he's done this to," Marlow told her.

"I'm so happy that you found her," Lola smiled. It was the first real smile he had seen from her since Walter's heart attack. "So, how can I help you?"

"See what you can find out about a man named Marcus Dawes."

"Why does that name sound familiar?" Lola looked

puzzled.

"His brother, Kurt, was Tina's stalker a while back," Marlow explained.

"How awful!" Lola gasped.

"It is for Tina, because it appears that Marcus is trying to take up where his brother left off.

"I'll certainly see what I can find," Lola told him.

"It can wait until tomorrow, Lola. Right now, it's time to call it a day. Are you staying here or at your apartment?" Marlow asked.

"I guess I will go to my place. It doesn't seem right staying here without Walter," Lola shook her head.

"Go get your stuff and I'll lock up and follow you home. With Dawes on the loose, I don't want to take any chances."

"Thank you, Rick," Lola told him, as she started gathering her things. Marlow went back to his office, set the alarm on his door, went to set the one on the front door before stepping outside behind Lola and locking it. He followed Lola to her car and then got in his own and followed Lola home. Once she was safely inside, he headed for his own apartment.

~ ~ ~

Tina and Jessica had decided to make supper. Rafael's stomach was growling loudly as he smelled the scents coming out of the kitchen. Still, when he heard a noise at the front door, Rafael was on his feet and moving to where he could cover the stairs with the shotgun. The door swung open and Marlow stood framed in the doorway. "Hey," Marlow said as he shut and locked the front door behind him.

"Good to see you," Cortez said.

"I can tell. Sam was right about you," Marlow said

"Sam's right about a lot of things."

"Smells like the girls are cooking."

"They are."

"Prepare yourself for a feast," Marlow grinned as he walked into the living room. He removed his .38 revolver from the holster and put it on the coffee table next to his favorite seat. Cortez returned to the chair he had been sitting on and laid the Mossberg across his knees, in a model of repose.

~ ~ ~

Oscar Christopher James sat quietly in the holding cell. It made the most sense to wait until the sheriff's department came to get him. His brother officers would be watching him too closely for him to do anything inside the station. But once he was in custody of the sheriff's department, they might be a bit more lax. If they were, then he would make his move and get away!

~ ~ ~

Rocco strolled along Mallory Square moving among the crowd like a ghost. He was searching for the big bastard that had broken his arm and given him the beat down. He had hoped to spot him in the crowd that came in everyday to watch the sunset, hoping to see the infamous green flash as the sun dipped into the sea. The flash was supposed to herald good luck for those that saw it. Of course, Rocco wasn't sure that the green flash was a real thing, but tonight he was too busy to watch for it. He was busy hunting for the man that had broken his arm and beaten him up.

On impulse, he headed toward Tina Cord's apartment. If the asshole had gone there once, maybe he would go there again. Except this time, he wouldn't be caught unaware. This time, he was prepared to fight back. He could feel the weight of the large ratchet tucked into the cargo pocket of the shorts he was wearing. The weight gave him a certain reassurance that this time, if he ran into the guy, things would be different!

"Ricky, I need to go to my apartment and get some more clothes. I really need to go back to work tomorrow," Tina said after supper was finished and the dishes had been done. Jessica had headed home, citing that she had early appointments the next day at her office.

"We can do that now," Marlow told her, leaning over to gently kiss her forehead.

"You want me to drive?" Rafael asked. Marlow looked at him.

"That might not be a bad idea. Two of us looking out for trouble improves our odds of avoiding it. They headed downstairs and Marlow stopped only long enough to lock his door and then he followed them out to Rafael's Dodge Charger and climbed inside. Rafael started the car and pulled out into the street.

~ ~ ~

Suddenly, Rocco stopped as he spotted the guy that had broken his arm. With his good hand he drew out the ratchet handle and gripped it tightly. He approached the guy as quietly as he could. Rocco raised his weapon and was getting ready to swing it down when the guy spun around with a meaty fist swinging out and crashing into Rocco's face, driving him backwards and off of his feet. Blood was running down his face and into his throat. The big cocksucker had broken his nose!

Rocco tried to scramble to his feet, but he wasn't fast enough. Dawes was on him in one stride and a heavy work boot crashed into his gut, lifting his whole body into the air. Rocco slammed to the ground, gasping for breath. "Stupid punk!" the big man snarled at him as his foot shot forward again. This time it caught Rocco in the face and his world went black. Marcus Dawes stood over him for a long moment. Then, he stomped down on his chest cracking his sternum, sending shards of bone into Rocco's heart. Stopping it from beating immediately. Rocco was dead. Dawes turned and carried his toolbox towards Tina Cord's front door.

~ ~ ~

Oscar James was completely compliant when he was escorted out of the police station and loaded into the back of a sheriff's department car. He smiled at the deputy as he fastened him in the seatbelt and shut the rear door. By the time the deputy put the car in motion, James had managed to slip the spare handcuff key that he carried out of a special pouch hidden inside his belt. It didn't take long to unlock the handcuffs and free his wrists.

James waited until they had left Stock Island and were heading north before leaning forward and drawing a boot knife that he wore inside his tactical boots. The officers that had searched him had missed it, as well, but that was okay because he had wanted them to miss it.

His fingers curled around the hilt of the knife as he dug the point into the fabric at the rear of the driver's seat. He made a long cut. He was counting on the noise of the police radio and the air conditioner to drown out the sound. James reached forward and removed stuffing and then he drove the blade forward hard, through the front of the seat and deep into the deputy's back. He felt the blade grind against bone and then the deputy slumped forward. His foot pressed on the gas and the car sped up, weaving all across the road until it hit the guard rail of the bridge and finally ground to a halt.

James kicked open the back window and reached out and opened the door from the outside. James scrambled out of the car and reached in and snatched the pistol from the dead deputy's belt. At least now, he was armed with more than just a knife. Oscar felt better already. He dragged the dead officer out of the car and rolled him over the rail and the body fell into the water below. Sharks would probably make short work of him. Oscar climbed into the driver's seat and restarted the car, continuing north. He would ditch the car in Miami along with his uniform. The cops would take care of Georgie. At long last, Oscar was free of the burden of his little brother once and for all!

~ ~ ~

Rafael pulled into a parking spot in front of Tina's apartment. "We all going in?" he asked.

"I think that might be a good idea," Marlow replied. Something was up and the small hairs at the back of his neck were standing on end.

"Ricky?" Tina asked, her voice suddenly small.

"Stay in the car," Marlow told her as he climbed out drawing his gun.

"What's going on?" Tina demanded.

"I don't know, yet," Marlow told her.

"Do you think Dawes is here?"

"I think that he might be," Marlow told her honestly.

"Then I want you to finish this, Ricky. Once and for all," Tina said.

"That is exactly what I plan to do," Marlow told her. Together, Marlow and Cortez started forward . . .

Chapter Nineteen

Marlow drew his revolver as he headed up the walk. Rafael was right behind him with a load of double-aught buckshot chambered in the Mossberg pump. As they drew closer, Marlow noticed that the door wasn't completely closed. He stopped. "What is it?" Rafael whispered from behind him.

"Somebody is inside," Marlow whispered over his shoulder.

"Do you think that it is Dawes?"

"I'd say that it's a good bet."

"What do you want to do?"

"We back off and call the cops, but we keep him inside," Marlow decided.

"Will that be enough for Tina?" Rafael asked quietly.

"It will have to be," Marlow said soberly. He pulled out his cell and dialed 9-1-1. When the dispatcher answered, Marlow identified himself, gave the address, and mentioned that the apartment in question had been broken into and that he thought the burglar was still inside.

"I've got two cars heading your way, Marlow. They will be running silent," the dispatcher told him.

"Roger that, I'll be waiting out front," Marlow told her

before hanging up.

"What's going on?" Tina asked, walking up behind them. Marlow turned to face her.

"Door is part way open. I think Dawes might be inside. I called the cops. If they can catch him in there, then they can hold him on breaking and entering with intent to commit a felony. He'll do hard time," Marlow assured her.

Just then, two Key West PD cars entered the parking lot and four cops climbed out. Marlow knew all of them. As they were approaching him, Tina's apartment exploded, sending bricks, glass, and flame shooting in all directions. They were all knocked to the ground by the force of the explosion.

Flames were rapidly spreading through the building as Marlow shoved himself to his feet and ran forward. He had to try and get as many people out as possible before the flame spread through the entire building. Flames were already shooting through holes in the roof. Marlow knew there was no hope for the lady that lived above Tina.

There were people already coming out from apartments farther away from the blast, and he could vaguely hear sirens over the ringing in his ears from the blast. Marlow helped people away from the building to a safe distance. It was several minutes before he went back to where he had left Tina and Rafael. They weren't there. Marlow began to get anxious. It wasn't like either of them to wander off. Had they decided to pitch in and help try to get people out of the building? Marlow started walking around, going to each group of folks that were standing and watching the fire department battle the blaze.

Still no sign of them. Marlow started back to where

Rafael had parked. He pulled out his cell and dialed Tina's cell. It went straight to voicemail. That couldn't be good. Just then he saw movement next to Rafael's car. It was a dazed looking Rafael climbing to his feet and holding his head. Blood was trickling from his hairline and a goose egg was forming. "Rafael what happened?" Marlow asked, rushing over to him.

"I got caught by surprise. Tina and I were starting forward to help and something crashed into my skull. I just woke up on the ground," Rafael replied, wincing.

"Tina's gone," Marlow told him.

"Rick, I'm sorry."

"Don't be. Dawes is fucking cunning. I bet he set that explosion off as soon as he saw me call the cops. He had me figured. He knew that I'd run to help get people out, and while you guys were distracted, he gave you a conk on the noggin and snatched Tina."

"It looks that way. What do we do now?"

"We find her and take care of this bastard once and for all," Marlow said, his face expressionless.

~ ~ ~

Walter Loomis was feeling weaker. He had put on a brave front for Lola because he knew it was it was the only way to get her to leave his side. His time on this earth was coming to an end. He had wanted to make Lola his wife before he died. They had accomplished that. He had also made sure that both Lola and Marlow would be well taken care of and would always have a place to work out of and call home.

Walter had known for several months that his health was failing. That was why he had cut back on his workload, so that he could spend more time with Lola. He had done everything he could to help Ricky straighten out his life as best he could. Tina Cord had helped on that score, too. He had been delighted when Ricky had met the young woman and they had been so smitten with each other.

It was getting harder to breathe. Walter could watch the blips of his heartbeat get farther apart. His time was drawing near. He had lived a good life. One that he was proud of. He closed his eyes for the last time and the line on the heart monitor went flat.

~ ~ ~

Marcus Dawes grinned as he looked over at the woman in the passenger seat. She was curled into a fetal position even though she was secured in the seatbelt. Grabbing her had been easy, almost too easy. When the bomb went off, Marlow had done exactly what he had thought the guy would do. He ran to help. The other guy with her had hesitated and gave him enough time to crack him on the head. He had snatched up Tina Cord and put her in a sleeper hold and dragged her back into the shadows. It didn't take long to reach his car and load her in. Now, it was time to take her to his rental place and exact his revenge on her for what she had done to his brothers!

He had rented his current residence with exacting his revenge in mind. It was at a fairly isolated location on Stock Island. It was well away from any prying neighbors. He would have all of the privacy he would need to make sure that Tina Cord would never cause trouble for him or his brother ever again.

~ ~ ~

"Thanks for coming, Jamie," Marlow told the chief

when he arrived in response to a call.

"What's going on, Marlow?"

"Tina's been kidnapped. Kurt Dawes brother blew up her apartment and snatched her while we were helping get people out of the building," Marlow explained.

"Okay, I'll get a BOLO out right away on Tina and this Dawes character," Chief Gutierrez said.

"Thanks. Meanwhile, Rafael and I are going to try and figure out where Dawes might have taken her," Marlow said.

"Call me if you find anything," Gutierrez told them.

"You'll be my first call," Marlow told him.

"Somehow, I doubt that," Jamie muttered as he walked off. He knew Marlow too well. If the man got a lead on where Tina might be, he wouldn't call Jamie until it was all over to give him plausible deniability.

~ ~ ~

Rafael was looking over the parking lot when he finally noticed something. There had been a pickup truck parked in the lot when they had arrived. It was gone now. It was the only vehicle missing out of the parking lot. He waved Marlow over. "I think I know what Dawes is driving," Rafael said.

"Talk to me," Marlow told him.

"There was a beat up pickup truck parked here when we got here."

"I remember seeing it."

"It is the only vehicle not here now."

"Meaning it was probably the vehicle Dawes is using," Marlow nodded. "I remember it had a faded sign painted on the side. I can't remember what it was though," Marlow shook his head.

"It was for a ranch of some kind," Rafael said.

"Let's get over to Stock Island. That's the only place in the Keys who would have any kind of ranch," Marlow said, heading for Rafael's car.

~ ~ ~

Marcus Dawes carried Tina Cord inside the old ramshackle building and put her down on a weathered wooden bench. She was still out from when she had fainted when he grabbed her. All the better. He would wake her up soon enough. Using bailing twine, Dawes tied her hands and feet to the boards of the table.

Unlike his brother Kurt, Marcus had no interest in women sexually. For him, it was all about the mutilation and torture. He walked over to a shelf and grabbed a metal bag that held his tools. He carried it over to the table and unfastened the clasp. He raised the lid and then reached in and pulled out an ampoule of smelling salts.

Thunder crashed outside, and rain started falling, rattling on the tin roof overhead. The weather forecasters hadn't been calling for thunderstorms tonight, but they often did spring up unexpectedly in the Keys. Marcus broke open the smelling salts and waved it under Tina's nose until her eyes jerked open and she tried to sit up, her eyes not yet focusing.

Finally, Tina's eyes did focus. Marcus Dawes grinned at her and it was an evil sight, promising pain and death. Tina screamed as loudly as she ever had. "Now, now, Miss Cord. I haven't even gotten started yet. We have a long night of fun ahead of us. So, please, save some screams for later," he told her laughing.

~ ~ ~

Lola Ponsberry Loomis had just returned to her apartment when the phone started ringing. She hesitated before walking over and picking it up. "Lola Ponsberry, I mean Loomis, speaking," she said. Lola hadn't bothered looking at the caller I.D. before answering but did so now and saw it was the hospital in Miami. All of the blood left her face.

"Mrs. Loomis? This is Doctor Schifrin. I was treating your husband," he said to give her a frame of reference.

"What do you mean, was?" Lola asked, tears welling up in   her   eyes. "Walter Loomis passed away this evening at approximately six o'clock. I'm sorry for your loss," the cardiologist told her.

Lola hung up, not believing what she had just heard. Walter was dead! He had lied to her, telling her that he was doing fine and would be home in a day or two. He had known that he was dying, and he had hidden that from her. Lola slowly dropped to her knees and put her hands to her face as she began to wail her sorrow to the night.

~ ~ ~

Marlow and Rafael cruised the streets of Stock Island trying to figure out where Dawes might have taken Tina. They were also looking for the old farm truck that had been parked in front of Tina's apartment before the bomb went off.

"I don't like this, Marlow. He could have taken her anywhere," Rafael sighed from the driver's seat. Marlow had Rafael's shotgun settled across his legs with the muzzle pointed towards the door on his right.

"I don't like it either, but here we are. The bastard got

her. All we can do is try to find her before it is too late," Marlow sighed. Lightning had been playing in the clouds above. Quickly, a bright bolt flashed in the sky and a thunderous boom followed it. That was when Marlow spotted the sign that was the same as the one on the side of the truck.

"Turn in there!" Marlow pointed just as the rain hit with blinding force.

Rafael flicked the wipers to full speed, but it was still hard to see out of the windshield as he followed the winding drive. As soon as his lights picked out the truck, he killed them and the engine, putting the Charger in park.

"What do we do now?" Rafael asked softly, already sure of what the answer would be.

"We go get Tina and put Dawes down like the rabid dog that he is," Marlow said as he pushed open his door and stepped out of the car. The rain was cold and wet and hard. It was also strangely invigorating after the heat of the day.

Running in a crouch, Marlow headed for the metal shack. He could see lights inside. His gut was churning with fear. His mouth tasted coppery with fear. He swallowed hard, hoping that they were not too late. He glanced over at Rafael Cortez. The big Cuban looked ready. He was just waiting on Marlow. A scream ripped the air coming out of the metal building. They could wait no longer! Marlow charged the building!

Chapter Twenty

Marcus had picked up a knife from his tool kit. He made sure to let Tina see it, to see how the light glinted off of the edge. He had spent hours honing it to razor perfection. He lowered the edge towards her face and she jerked away making him laugh. Instead of using it to cut her flesh, Marcus began to cut away her clothing, stripping it from her, along with any shred of dignity that she might imagine that she had left.

Tina struggled against the twine that bound her wrists and ankles. She was more afraid than she had ever been while Marcus Dawes cut away her clothing. She could only imagine what he might do next and that frightened her even more.

After he had removed her clothing, he tossed the rags into a corner. "Are you ready, baby? The fun is just beginning," Marcus told her. "Now, where should we start?" He kept the sharp scalpel hovering just above her skin as he moved around her body. Tina was biting her lip trying to believe that Marlow would find her in time.

"Please, don't do this," Tina sobbed, hating herself for begging this monster.

"Oh, now, none of that, Tina. You are responsible for

two of my brothers going to jail. One of them is dead now because of you. Don't you feel the least bit guilty about that? You should, you know. Because it was entirely your fault!" Marcus said as he stabbed the scalpel into her arm.

Tina screamed as he twisted the scalpel. Then his other hand moved to her crotch and she could feel his finger roughly pushing inside her. Tina screamed again, a long drawn out wail.

~ ~ ~

Marlow flattened himself against the side of the shack. He knew that Rafael was close behind him. The rain was falling heavier now, plastering his hair and clothing against his skin. He heard Tina scream again, this one long and drawn out. He spun away from the wall and ran to the door kicking it in as he reached it and racing inside.

The lights were bright, and he squinted against them as he charged inside. He could see that Tina was naked and bleeding on the table. He lifted his .38 and fired. Marcus Dawes jerked back, snarling a curse as blood sprayed from his left shoulder. Dawes jerked the scalpel out of Tina's arm and threw it at Marlow like a knife.

Marlow ducked and fired again. This time the bullet struck Dawes in the leg. Dawes grabbed a large knife and charged at Marlow. He kicked out with his good leg catching Marlow's wrist and sending the revolver flying. Marlow stepped inside, driving a hard elbow into Dawes' mouth. Blood sprayed from lips mashed against teeth.

A rock hard fist crossed Marlow's jaw knocking him back against the corrugated tin wall. He was seeing double as Dawes raced for him. Marlow put everything he had into a hard kick to the groin. His foot connected with Dawes and lifted him off of the floor. Dawes collapsed to the floor with both hands going to his crotch, vomit spraying from his mouth.

Marlow kicked Dawes again. This time in the side of the head and he collapsed to the floor no longer moving. Marlow staggered to the table and started untying Tina. Once her hands were free, she threw her arms around him and held on tightly while Marlow lifted her off the table. He had just turned around when he saw that Dawes was no longer on the floor. Marlow put Tina down, shoving her behind him.

Dawes slashed at him with a hunting knife that Marlow only just avoided. Dawes slashed again before Marlow could go on the attack. Marlow backed up keeping himself between Tina and the insane killer.

Dawes kept coming, shifting his hunting knife from left to right hand as he pushed forward. Marlow kept a wary eye on him frantically searching for something, anything he could use as a weapon to could go on the offensive.

Thunder crashed outside, sounding like the roar of Armageddon. Marlow wondered what had happened to Rafael. Did Dawes have friends helping him? He hoped not. He would have a hell of a time explaining it to Sam if anything happened to Cortez.

"I'm going to rip your guts out and I'm going to make sure she watches you die before I kill her. And I can tell you, she will die screaming," Dawes grinned a bloody smile. "Because while she watches you die, I am going to be skinning her alive!" Dawes cackled like a man who had totally lost his mind.

"I don't think so," said an accented voice from behind

Dawes. The madman turned to see Rafael standing in the doorway holding the 12-guage in his hand.

"Who the fuck are you?" Dawes asked.

"The end of you," Rafael smiled. Flame erupted from the 12-guage along with a charge of double-aught buckshot. It hit Dawes in the face and disintegrated his head in a splash of crimson and bone and gray matter. Dawes' body tumbled to the floor minus his head.

"About time you got here," Marlow grinned.

"I got held up by traffic," Rafael Cortez replied with a grin of his own. Marlow pulled out his cellphone and dialed 9-1-1. He requested both an ambulance for Tina and detectives from the sheriff's department.

~ ~ ~

The storm was starting to let up as Tina was taken to the Lower Keys Medical Center. Marlow and Rafael were both being questioned by sheriff's department personnel and the FDLE. Chief Jamie Gutierrez was there, as well.

~ ~ ~

By the time the police were done with them, and Marlow and Rafael got to the Lower Keys Medical Center, Jessica Harmon was already there and with Tina. Tina's wound had been bandaged and she had been sedated. She was resting when Marlow walked into her room. "How is she?" Marlow asked.

"In shock. This was a major setback, Rick. Tina was in a somewhat delicate state of mind after testifying against Dawes brother in Chicago. After what she had been going through, being stalked again by Marcus Dawes, and what he did to her, she's retreated into herself," Jessica told him softly.

"Meaning what, Jess?"

"It means, the shock of this on top of the other incidents, may have drastic and unexpected results. Tina may never quite be herself again." Marlow dropped into a chair. His face went suddenly pale.

His cell phone started ringing and he snatched it up, answering it as he tried to process what Dr. Harmon had just told him. "Marlow," he answered.

"Rick, Walter died earlier tonight," Lola's voice filled his ear.

"What?" Marlow gasped. If he hadn't already been sitting, he would have collapsed.

"I tried calling you earlier, but you didn't answer," Lola told him.

"I was trying to rescue Tina from Marcus Dawes," Marlow's voice was barely above a whisper.

"Will you go up to Miami with me tomorrow to claim the body? I don't think I can do this alone," Lola sobbed.

"Yes, I'll go with you," Marlow said, hanging up the phone.

"What's going on, Rick?" Jessica asked.

"Walter's dead. His heart gave out earlier this evening. Lola wants me to go with her to claim his body tomorrow," Marlow explained.

"I'll stick around and watch over Tina," Rafael offered.

"Thank you, thank you both. I need to go," Marlow said, forcing himself to his feet and hurrying out of the room. Rafael took the seat that Marlow had just vacated. Nobody would hurt Tina Cord on his watch. He looked at Doctor Harmon.

"What did you mean when you said that she has

retreated into herself, Doc?" Rafael asked.

~ ~ ~

A cool breeze was blowing in off the ocean now that the storm had passed. Marlow was sweating as he plunged out of the hospital into the night. His whole body was shaking. He needed a cigarette and he needed a drink. Walter dead? It couldn't be! How had he not seen it coming? How could he have missed how sick Walter had to have been?

His head was reeling. Marlow called a taxi and took it home. Misty wound around his feet when he entered his apartment, but he ignored her, heading straight to the kitchen. Marlow grabbed the bottle of vodka from the freezer and uncapped it, taking a long pull straight from the bottle, and carried it to the living room. He punched in a jazz CD disc into his player and took another long pull on the bottle as the music began to swell out of the speakers.

It didn't take long for him to pass out. When he did, his sleep was dark and dreamless. He didn't wake up until the early morning sun was streaming through the blinds.

His mouth felt like cotton and his head felt like and oversized bowling ball. He looked at his watch. It was barely five a.m. Marlow pushed himself to a sitting position on the couch. His stomach rolled, and he scrambled into the bathroom to void his stomach into the toilet.

His forehead was beaded with sweat when he finally stopped heaving. He climbed off the floor to his feet and went to change into his running shorts and a tank top. He slipped his house key into his pocket and headed down stairs and out the door which he locked behind him. Then, Marlow started to run.

He ran until he could feel the alcoholic daze burn away

in the sweat coming out of his pores. He covered two miles before turning and heading back to his apartment. By the time he returned home, he felt better. He showered and dressed and then he went out and got in his car and drove to the office. He figured that Lola would go there first, as well. Marlow put on coffee as soon as he arrived, and the smell was filling the building when Lola unlocked the front door and stepped inside. Marlow handed her a cup of coffee. "Talk to me," Marlow told her.

"What am I going to do, Ricky?" Lola asked him.

"Walter made arrangements for us both. Do you want to continue working for me?" Marlow asked.

"I need a job," Lola admitted.

"As Walter's wife, this house is yours if you want it. It is paid for and the utilities are taken care of for the next five years. If you don't want it, it goes to me, but there is a trust set up to pay you your current wage until you are old enough to retire. Hiram told me that," Marlow explained.

Lola shook her head. "I wouldn't feel right living here without him. How is Tina?"

"Tina might never recover. Jessica says that she has retreated into herself. She isn't responding to any outside stimulus," Marlow sighed.

"Oh, Ricky, I am so sorry," Lola told him.

"It is what it is, Lola. Walter wanted us to lean on each other if anything happened to him. So, given that, will you stay on as my secretary and girl Friday?" Marlow asked her.

"I'll do that, yes," Lola replied.

"Too many people have died, Lola. Walter, Rocco, and Tina is lost in her mind. Thank you for being here for me."

"Of course, I am Rick, just as you are here for me."

179

Lost Girl

~ ~ ~

Surprisingly, Walter's funeral was held on a very bright and sunny day two days later. The sky above was clear and a bright blue. Marlow and Lola stood near the coffin as the preacher gave the final sermon. Thom Hark and Rafael Cortez were there, as well, along with a good number of Walter's friends and clients.

Marlow could barely listen to the preacher when he gave his sermon at the graveside. His mind wandered back over the years. All of the years that he had known 'Uncle Walter' as a friend of the family. Walter, who had taken him in after his father had been murdered in the line of duty. Walter who had given him a chance after everyone else had written him off. The preacher finished his sermon and the crowd began to disperse. Everyone, except for Marlow and Lola. Both of them lagged behind. Each of them tossed a handful of dirt onto the casket. Then, they walked together to the limo that would take them back to the office.

~ ~ ~

Oscar Christopher James never reached Miami. He was struck and killed by a hit and run driver while trying to hitch a ride on the narrow bridges leading back to the mainland. Sheriff's deputies delivered the news to Quinn Kerns and her mother.

Thank you for reading.
Please review this book. Reviews help others find
Absolutely Amazing eBooks and inspire us to keep
providing these marvelous tales.

If you would like to be put on our email list to
receive updates on new releases, contests, and
promotions, please go to AbsolutelyAmazingEbooks.com
and sign up.

About the Author

Bill Craig is the best-selling author of more than 60 novels spread across the genres from mystery to pulp to science fiction to westerns. Bill is best know for his Marlow Key West mysteries and his Mitch Cooper mysteries. Bill often likes to say that it only took him 34 years to become an overnight success. And when introducing himself he adds that he kills people for a living, much like the fictional Rick Castle on television.

Marlow will return in ...

Marlow: Red Tide

When a dead fisherman is found floating in the waters off of Smathers Beach, the U.S. Coastguard writes it off as an accident. But when his wife is found dead under suspicious circumstances two days later, his sister hires Rick Marlow to look into it. But as Marlow begins his investigation, more bodies begin to drop, and Marlow must find out why before Key West is washed away in a Red Tide of blood!

ABSOLUTELY AMAZING eBOOKS

AbsolutelyAmazingEbooks.com
or AA-eBooks.com